# BLUE HEART

## Book 3: Gods & Assassins

### Frank Kennedy

# Dedicated to everyone who can't resist shiny things

c. 2023 by Frank Kennedy
All rights reserved
ISBN: 9798857904466

**A note from the author:**

This is Book 3 of a serialized story. Please read the first two before you jump in here. *Gods & Assassins* is set in the universe of the Collectorate, which includes at least two other series. Reading them is not a prerequisite. However, if you want a wider look at the Collectorate, please check out those offerings.

I'd love for you to become part of my literary family. Sign up for my newsletter, which drops every three weeks along with free books and special offers. You can also follow me on Facebook, where you'll find me hanging out daily. Come on over and let's chat!

# 1

**Collectorate Standard Year (SY) 5389**

TEAM. A sweet word that morphed by each new sunrise. For two thousand years, it was Moon and me. Now there were six compatriots at the table of absolute trust, with others nearing graduation. The underpinning for our galactic army of criminals and general mischief-makers was solidifying.

Today, we sought to eliminate a significant obstacle on the road to expanding our influence. Not the last one by a long damn shot, but the most immediate.

That need brought us to Machado, famously known as a 'walking city.' Aside from the public tube transports and shuttles, this collection of nearabout a million people wove together a nice web of pedestrian bridges and moving sidewalks. The streets and parking it afforded for private sedans like Bart were sufficient, but the local tradition put feet before Carbedyne fins. My team designed around those logistics.

The calculations proved far more cumbersome than defending the road train. Machado's convoluted infrastructure forced us to take into account a wide range of variables. Of top importance: Enter and leave the city with the same level of anonymity.

Blend in.

Watch the time.

Avoid the secure drones.

These protocols would've been rendered moot if Moon and I assaulted a Cardinale business or homestead at thirty times the speed of humans, guns blazing. A slaughterfest. Ample mayhem kept folks distracted long enough for a clean getaway.

Yeah, no. This mission required a subtle touch. We lived in a different world since the attack on Road Train 1492. The public knew nothing of what happened twenty days ago on Roadway 9; the Montez Shipping Group and their contacts in the constabulary saw to it. Aztecans need not fear the rise of pirates. Yet.

The public learned about the shocking assassination of Senora Evelyn Cardinale and her entourage by an unnamed rival cartel. Though the tiny militia of Desperido had not reached cartel status, I appreciated the compliment – and the disinformation.

Another massive assault on Horax interests likely couldn't be covered up so effectively, which meant today's effort required a more surgical approach.

I crossed the Atrejo Gardens Bridge with my so-called bodyguard, Elian. He and I wore dark, inconspicuous suits which screamed, "Nothing here to see! Move along!" However, my upturned collar and red scarf in the breast pocket elevated me on the corporate hierarchy. Elian dyed his spikes black and trimmed his beard to a well-manicured goatee. He hid his eyes behind narrow black lenses.

I designed my temporary identity based on a single word: Nondescript. A dull man with no sense of humor, tiny but alert eyes behind wire-frame glasses, gelled black hair parted down the middle, slender nose, and a double chin. He hid his hands in the lower pockets of his tailored jacket and never allowed anyone to distract him from his destination.

A serious man for whom no one cared a wit.

Perfect.

I created my new shape without assistance from Theo, who preferred to wax poetic about the moral implications of today's mission rather than the practical needs. I longed for the stubborn bastard who used to criticize me at every turn. His "evolved state" – Theo's words, not mine – forced him to confront what it meant to be a *D'ru-shaya,* or so he claimed.

Theo embraced Addis's echo into his matrix despite my strict orders to punt the bitch. I rarely survived two hours without hearing a diatribe from those minor-league moralists.

The bridge's foot traffic moved both ways at a steady pace, with a healthy mix of office workers and their administrators. The Atrejo Financial District was the place where power clashed with people who could only dream of it. As someone who used to have more power than anyone in the nine universes, I snickered at these delusional assholes. Their notion of 'power' was an office upstairs.

Eh. Petty goals for short-timers.

Whatever happened to real ambition? As in, "I'd like to conquer this star system!"

Tyrants and other garden-variety megalomaniacs tended to be controversial, but history did not forget them. And before they arrived at their typically violent demise? Those bastards lived it up.

I respected people with vision. Even now, somewhere in the Collectorate – close to the President's side, most likely – a man codenamed Q6 was organizing a multi-planetary rebellion against the established order. My last intel suggested the plan might be years from fruition, which indicated Q6 savored each step in the larger scheme. He took a shine to the strategic maneuvers as much as the outcome.

These folks crisscrossing the Atrejo Gardens Bridge?

Placeholders. Cogs. Gene stamps on personnel data spools.

Yet, I supposed the job gave these mortals a sense of purpose. Who was I to demean?

Elian nudged me as we cut a clean path through the unsuspecting suits and blouses.

"I remember this bridge, boss."

"How so, my friend?"

"See the third tower over your left shoulder? Snead Biotech."

I noticed without slowing my pace.

"Ah. Where you hit your low-water mark."

"That's the one. Security escorted me all the way out here. One malgado said he'd toss me over if I showed my face again."

"You've come far, Elian." I tapped my ear bead. "Status, Ilan?"

"I'll have a visual in two minutes."

Moon sounded upbeat, which was far distant from his original assessment of my mission proposal. He didn't appreciate stepping into a subordinate role, with Elian taking his place at my side. Moon's attitude adjusted when I convinced him to approach his job as if he were assassinating for the President.

"More important," I reminded him, "Elian is not a shapeshifter. He wouldn't make it out of the city alive."

"I'll get it done, partner."

After which, he chose a more docile appearance for this venture. We hadn't polished so well since Qasi Ransome, now sixty standard days in our rear view.

"Ship," I said over the bead, "what's the view from your end?"

"Quiet, boss," the kid replied from inside Bart. "We haven't raised any alarms."

"Excellent. How long until you move?"

"Eleven minutes, forty seconds."

I certified Ship on the sedan's Nav a week ago. Though he didn't take to the holo interface as speedily as Elian or Saul, our other new Nav, Ship practiced nonstop.

"Keep us alert to any changes, my friend. Stay on schedule."

"Will do, boss."

We crossed the bridge and descended spiral stairs. Below and beyond, the Atrejo Memorial Gardens snaked through the financial district, featuring a fine collection of indigenous flora. Everything from spiral cacti to bayonet-leaf oaks.

Water features. Contemplative music from hidden speakers. Artificial aromatics. The works.

At the eastern end – two city blocks away – the children's park.

Our destination.

"Stay alert," I told Elian. "But not a word."

"Gotcha, boss."

I gave Elian a challenging role based on the premise 'less is more.' We rehearsed body language and the art of stoicism.

"Give away nothing, my friend. Broad shoulders. Stare through them, not at them. Their imagination will take control, leaving you with the advantage."

Elian was a quick study with a brilliant mind. A little psychotic, perhaps. Sometimes driven by reckless emotion.

Normal human traits.

We strolled through the gardens at a casual pace. I rubbed my hand against the low-hanging branch of a puffer tree and unleashed a cloud of tiny white petals. My olfactory sensors, at their most delicate, smelled a perfume too subtle for human noses. I thought of a first whiff of white wine after popping the cork.

It reminded me of the last time I sipped wine – the Club Moulet on Qasi Ransome. Nice.

I had no intention of echoing that job's fiery conclusion in the center of Machado. But it wasn't off the table; our target would choose for us.

"I've acquired our man," I told the team. "Ilan?"

"I have a visual on my target," Moon said. "Sending to your pom."

"Excellent. Time to close the deal."

The children's playground featured the tried and true: A gym for kids under six. Climb, run, chase, slide. And sand. Lots of sand.

Parents and friends watched their little ones from benches at the park's end. *Watch* might've been an exaggeration. Most scrolled the holos of their poms.

Not our target, however.

He sat alone on a bench for two, following the little ones' pursuits with a contented smile. His bodyguards blended in with the civilians, but they wouldn't make a move unless I provoked them. Per our training, Elian stepped away as I approached the target.

I retrieved my pom and halted near the bench. Our man didn't notice me – or perhaps he let such matters fall to his security. I saw bliss on a withered face that recently experienced great loss. He was sixty-three, but the heavy bags and the silver hair spoke of a man heading toward the sunset.

Still, I recognized those blue eyes. He gave them to his son Vash, the kid he never knew.

"Joy is a child's laughter," I said.

Mateo Cardinale didn't respond. No surprise. I raised my volume.

"I miss the innocence. We lose it so early."

My new shape spoke with a cultured air. He was, I decided, a man of few words who preferred to listen before springing a verbal trap. Senor Cardinale diverted his gaze.

"You have children here?" He asked.

Time to engage the empathy snare.

"I used to. A son."

"Grown?"

"I lost him in the Swarm war."

The target stiffened his jowls.

"Condolences."

"Nineteen years ago. You have children, senor?"

Cardinale grunted his pleasure.

"The best kind. Grandchildren. I can love them until they exhaust me, then I return them to their parents."

He laughed at his joke while I opened my pom.

"You watch them while their parents work?"

His lines softened. Cardinale was warming to me.

"No, no. Two hours is all these old bones can manage."

That matched our intel exactly. He brought them here five days a week. Same time. On the hour.

I turned to him and extended my pom.

"I'd like to show you an image." No one in Cardinale's vicinity moved, but I detected at least three sets of eyes keenly observe. "I don't wish to overstep."

He unfolded his arms in a gesture of welcome, no doubt a signal to keep his entourage at bay.

"Your son?" He asked.

"A boy."

I tore off the holo transmitting from Moon's location and shoved it toward Cardinale. His features hardened like an ice sculpture the instant he saw the projection. His eyes wanted to signal rage and alert his people to the clear and present danger.

Yeah, no. This fella knew how to behave.

Terror held his anger in check.

"May I sit?" I asked while proceeding to do just that.

"If you lay a hand on Rafa ..."

The seventeen-year-old in the holo lounged poolside with a gaggle of similar boys. Moon didn't have to penetrate the private club's security to produce a closeup image. The sighter drone he launched did the work.

"Your grandson is safe, Senor Cardinale. For now."

"What in ten hells do you want?"

I trained my eyes on the little ones.

"Your family is your legacy."

"My family will not be used as a bargaining chip."

Good. He sensed where I was headed.

"You've traveled this road, Senor Cardinale."

He knew better than to raise his voice.

"You have crossed a tragic line."

I focused on the holo.

"What I have done is gain your attention."

"For what purpose?"

Ah. Now to business.

"You have not fallen in line."

Rafa Cardinale jumped into the pool with his mates.

"You're with Montez?"

"I have many clients, Senor Cardinale. They're impatient."

"I made my position clear. No threat will change it."

I sighed with a mild disappointment that suggested his response had been predicted. Time to escalate.

"When my clients become impatient, they send me."

"Tell your clients: My family's enterprise will not bear the sole blame. I can also send a man. Your clients also have families."

"With one notable exception. Theirs are protected."

"If they make a move against …"

I cut him off with a demonstrative finger.

"We can eliminate your legacy with a moment's notice."

Moon spoke in my ear: "In position."

"Mateo, please observe."

The man's first name was my signal to Moon.

I expanded the holo so the new patriarch of the Horax might see the full scope of the event.

Moon appeared as a blur, from which emerged carefully targeted laser bolts. The raucous good time in that pool turned docile.

Teenage bodies floated quietly on the water but for one.

Rafa Cardinale flailed amid the corpses of his friends.

"No. Rafa. I will kill …"

Elian was prepared if Mateo overreacted. He'd been trained how to anticipate the man's bodyguards. No moment in our mission posed greater danger. If Mateo turned on me …

"Rafa is unharmed." I burrowed my eyes into him and buried my voice to a seething whisper. "For the moment. We can eliminate your family *now*."

He pressed a hand against his chest. If the man had a heart condition, this seemed a reasonable time for it to emerge.

"What … w-what is it you want?"

"Full capitulation. The Horax will accept sole blame for violation of Aztecan piracy law. You will withdraw your spies from Montez and the shipping guilds. You will concede all territory east and south of Machado. If you violate these terms, we will erase the Cardinale name from history."

His sunken eyes screamed defeat, but Mateo wasn't done.

"You won't escape justice. I'll track you to the ends of Azteca."

"Senor Cardinale, you lost a sister but gained what was rightfully yours. Take the prize and walk."

I threw away the holo and closed my pom.

"Your grandson will need comfort in his time of grief."

The second most dangerous moment followed: Our departure.

I rose, wondering whether he'd try to make a stupid move. One signal to his entourage would turn these gardens into a second site of carnage. Why commit suicide in front of his grandchildren?

"Stand, Senor Cardinale. Take my hand."

He'd have a difficult damn time explaining that image off a secure-drone feed while accusing me of threatening his family.

Naturally, he refused.

"Miserable malgado. Leave while you can."

My hand remained extended.

"If I leave unsatisfied, the worst will follow. Capitulate and enjoy the laughter of children."

What choice did he have?

Power is as good as the next asshole in the pecking order. I was that asshole.

Mateo Cardinale, father of nine and grandfather to twenty, chose to live another day. I gripped his hand like a steel claw; not enough to break bones.

I wanted him to remember the moment for the rest of his life.

"Good man." I leaned in for added effect. "You have one standard day to settle these affairs. We will be watching."

As I turned, the shaken old fella mustered enough energy to ask:

"Who are you?"

I stifled a grin but waited for inspiration.

"Pray you never know."

I stowed my pom and hid my hands inside the pockets. If these fools intended to defy me from behind, I had just cut my reaction time by four-tenths of a second. Risky.

Elian held his position as I walked past, lending his eyes to the enemy. He'd retreat when I was thirty meters clear.

The job wasn't done; a few deft maneuvers lay ahead. Nonetheless, I took pride in my performance.

Words first, then guns. A lovely combination.

# 2

**M**OON AND I HAD NEVER BEEN SLOWER. After I absorbed his reserves during the attack on Road Train 1492, we lost forty percent of our footspeed. We still brought enough juice to overwhelm all comers in a straight-up gun battle, but an enemy with the proper tech might track us with a predictive algorithm. A finely honed network of secure drones could isolate our movements and develop a profile.

That reality factored into our Machado escape strategy. We planned routes that skirted most of the city's network, even if they absorbed valuable time. It wasn't a new idea. We employed it to a lesser degree during our ten-day visit to Qasi Ransome.

Elian and I split up at the western end of the gardens. I proceeded north, away from our rendezvous point, while he turned south. We used public water rooms where a change of clothes had been stowed. His transformation, I suspect, was less painful.

I emerged as a young man with luscious locks, earrings, amber contact lenses, and a form-fitting muscle shirt. I wasn't entirely out of place: Fellas like him were known to prowl the financial district servicing clients. Though I carried a magnetic sexual appeal, the template did not form easily, and every synthetic muscle burned. My weaker syneth core didn't take kindly to shifting from Raul Torreta twice in a day.

I gave the secure drones a few looks at my temporary beauty then dashed through the unmonitored zones at top speed, leaving a string of puzzled locals in my wake.

Ship guided Bart into the third level of a residential parking lodge a kilometer south of where we disembarked. I rendezvoused seconds ahead of Moon, who had shifted into an old bald man in a jumpsuit. He based the template on someone he assassinated during our first job for the President.

"Well done, Ship," I said when we entered Bart. "Perfectly timed."

"Thanks, boss. It was all in the planning. Followed the script."

I slapped him on the shoulder.

"Next time, perhaps, we'll send you into the field, my friend, and Elian can handle Nav."

"Can't wait. Got to admit, I was excited watching it play out. And you, Ilan? That was a damn sight to behold. I replayed the pool attack twice. Slowed it down to catch your technique. You're too fast."

Moon acknowledged the kid with a sharp nod, but it was a courtesy. Slaughtering a gaggle of kids in a swimming pool was simple fare. He also had no time for compliments – like me, Moon craved a comfortable template. He undressed at the wardrobe where Ilan Natchez's ensemble awaited.

Seconds after Moon, I reached into my syneth core and visualized the man who lived on Azteca for nineteen years. My biology revised until Raul Torreta – the most suave malgado on the Naugista Plateau – replaced the unnamed male prostitute.

"Reckon I'll never get used to that," Ship said after watching us shapeshift. "I've been meaning to ask: Does it hurt?"

I glanced at Moon, hoping he'd engage the kid. He was too busy reassembling Ilan's attire.

"Pain is relative, my friend. This is familiar skin, so it's a relief. The others can pose a challenge."

Ship and Elian adjusted to working for gods with stunning ease. Ship had known from the start I wasn't human, so nothing shocked him when Moon revealed our shapeshifting ability the night after we won the battle on Roadway 9. Moon gave each lieutenant a cigar from his special stock and allowed them to help incinerate the eighty-four Horax fools who we electrocuted. When Moon returned home, he said neither one was repulsed by the task and that Elian was downright giddy. Over the following days, Elian peppered us with questions about the science of syneth and our voluminous backstory, but we doled out answers in small, innocuous bites.

Our true names? Too soon.

How we became gods? They'd never understand.

Our adventures across the nine universes? Not for years, if they lived so long.

Why we were forced to take human form? Too painful.

We silenced their questions with two critical revelations:

One: We were professional assassins who worked for a privileged client and amassed wealth to someday form the largest criminal syndicate in the history of the human race. We wanted Elian and Ship at our sides.

Two: If they ever betrayed our confidence to anyone, we would kill them instantly.

Each reacted as any ambitious human might when offered the chance to become a top general of a grand and nefarious empire.

"All I have to do is keep my mouth shut? Where do I sign?"

Humans in need of respect and purpose were infinitely malleable.

"Elian, how much farther?"

"Parking lodge in sight, boss."

"Any problems en route?"

"Nothing but glitter."

I turned to Moon, who finished dressing and lit a cigar.

"What do you think? Will my instincts prove spot-on? Or, as Elian would say, 'nothing but glitter'."

He retrieved a liquor bottle and a glass.

"Hard to say, partner. Depends on who the five dead kids are."

That was the one unforeseen variable. We knew the grandson and his social circle of spoiled-ass-rotten rakes spent most of their carefree days at Machado's most exclusive club. Productivity was not on their agenda. They lured other privileged parasites from a wide assortment of families who reveled in perceived power. If sons of close associates to the Cardinales floated in that pool, no problem. But if one happened to be, say, the son of an Aztecan representative to the Interstellar Congress ...

Yeah, the entire region would feel the blowback.

"We'll have our answer in the coming days. It's a process, my friend. And, I hope, the close of an important chapter."

Moon poured a glass for both of us and handed me a stout whiskey.

"Agree, partner. It's time to move on to the next phase."

Moon handled the past twenty days of incremental progress with surprising aplomb. He didn't kill anyone in Desperido to force my hand; that in itself was an improvement. He put greater effort into training the militia. At least once a day, someone caught him smiling.

Brief, mind you. Blink-and-you-miss-it brief. Urban-legend brief.

Still, an upgrade.

Theo, now an amateur psychologist, attributed Moon's agreeability to Elian and Ship's acceptance of his godhood.

*"It's our opinion,"* he said, referring to himself and Addis, *"that Moon seeks validation from humans, much as he did when he was a mortal. As you know, his relationship with his father Bonju was often strained. He used to speak at great length to Addis about those early years. In one sense, he is still experiencing the pangs of childhood in this new life as a fallen god."*

And on and on he rambled, despite my succinct retorts.

"The man is no child, metaphorically or otherwise, Theo. He's killed billions of humans. Destroyed whole planets. Why can't you settle for a short, nasty broadside?"

"How unfair. Surely, a man is more than the sum of a cheap insult."

And there it was. A *D'ru-shaya* that specialized in reflection.

I didn't know how good I had it before a Horax malgado almost killed me on the tumbler.

When Elian joined us onboard, he removed his shoulder-length brown wig and ocean blue contact lenses. I grabbed two more glasses, and Moon poured our lieutenants a double shot. I offered a toast:

"Teamwork. We do not succeed without it. Everyone carried off his role to perfection."

Elian threw back his whiskey and licked his lips.

"It went down like you said, boss. You and Ilan sent a message they won't forget. So clean."

"What's today's lesson, my friend?"

The Motif master winked.

"The three P's: Preparation, patience, and poise. They'll win the mission every time. Overlook one, and you're a dead man."

"Were you ever tempted to break character?"

Elian chuckled. "Every second after we entered the park. Good thing I listened to my teachers. Nobody's mastered the game like them. Right, Ship?"

The kid spent years serving liquor, but drinking was another matter. Our favorite brand didn't sit well with his gut. Ship nodded in obvious discomfort.

Eh. He'd adapt in time.

"Never forget, my friends. The actual assassination plays a brief role in any mission. It can be little more than an afterthought if the quiet elements are performed to their peak."

"Yeah, boss. Don't move until you hold the winning hand."

"Agree, Ship?"

"For sure, boss. Strike when the time's right for you, not them."

I shared a grin with my compatriots at Ship's expense. He didn't look well at all.

"Whatcha think, kid? Can you pilot Bart home?"

He tried – poorly – to hide his discomfort but soldiered on.

"No worries," he said, taking a seat at the Nav. That sigh said he was glad to be off his feet. "Ready, boss."

I could've given him a break, but what lesson would that have taught? Instead, I offered Elian the co-pilot's seat. Moon and I played silent observers, much like we had during daily training flights.

Ship fumbled through the holocontrols at first but got a grip on the return flight plan. With a small assist from the AI, he guided us through this labyrinthine city, past the enforcement patrols, and onto an overland course. We entered the lightly populated Killamano Mountain Range forty kilometers west of Machado, throwing off any curious assholes who might try to predict our destination.

Ship engaged the worm drive. The usual buckle when we entered the aperture likely did the kid's belly no favors. Yet he was motivated to impress; a sore tummy wasn't about to interfere.

Two weeks earlier, I took him to space, where he stared out at Azteca from the same vantage Elian did on his first jaunt. It was a short visit; Ship was not awestruck. He asked one question.

"How long before we leave the system, Raul?"

"A year, more or less. Assuming all the pieces fall into place."

He contemplated my answer and sighed with obvious relief.

"I'll be seventeen. I used to think I'd be stranded on Azteca for the rest of my life."

"Pouring drinks in the cantina?"

He swallowed. "With a rusted claw."

The kid usually avoided tears, but his eyes were wet when I catalyzed the worm drive for the return trip. I flipped the holo his way and pointed out which control to tap.

"Your first unregistered jump. Remember it, kid."

He celebrated the moment with a generous grin.

"Just like the day you strolled into town and asked for a tour. Changed my life, boss."

Twelve standard days later, he exited Bart five hundred meters south of Desperido. Couldn't have asked for better from the kid.

He brought the sedan to a smooth landing, where a handful of our militia waited for news. Genoa and Saul, the most recent additions to our trusted inner table, greeted us first. They supervised the town's defense in our absence.

Genoa was what you might call silent but deadly. She allowed her ice-cold gaze, tri-colored crew cut, and teardrop tattoo to make the necessary first impression. She learned by listening, which I always found refreshing among humans. In a few short weeks, she developed the steadiest trigger outside of Moon and I. She distinguished herself while defending Road Train 1492; Genoa took out more targets while using a third the package of laser bolts.

I never used to concern myself with such metrics. My philosophy bent toward, "If you got 'em, shoot 'em." Overwhelming force.

These days, our resources were leaner. We had more than enough weapons, but Moon and I couldn't manufacture the firing bolts willy-nilly with our limited syneth. And, as we discovered in recent weeks, the cartels maintained a tight grip on arms smuggling. One avenue remained open, but negotiations in that corner had proved troublesome.

My next order of business: Up the ante with Lumen and those damn Children of Orpheus.

"We should soon see a full resolution to the Cardinale problem," I told Genoa, Saul, and the other militia. "Mission accomplished. What of Desperido?"

"Quiet, boss," Genoa said. "No surprise inquisitions today."

Constabulary and Montez investigators paid Desperido a few visits after the tumbler attack. The town responded with a well-rehearsed rebuttal to all suspicions and/or accusations:

*Militia? What militia? You must have heard wrong. We're a peaceful little desert town with nothing to offer but red dust on our shoes. Visit our cantina if you're thirsty.*

To be fair, no one pressed hard for answers. The functionaries they sent filled a checklist role. All parties – except the Horax, who took the fall – wanted the matter silenced in a damn hurry.

Genoa, who joined the militia at Elian's suggestion – she had worked on his Motif squad for months – learned the truth about her bosses ten days after Elian and Ship. Elian insisted Genoa could be trusted; she shared his desire to see Motif spread to all forty planets and also wanted adventure beyond Azteca. When I reminded him of the consequence for rejecting our truth or betraying it to others, Elian took full responsibility and vowed to kill Genoa himself, if necessary.

Genoa cracked a smile that day and said:

"Sold."

And I used to think nobody respected gods!

One man deduced what we were through observation. That's how Saul joined the table of trust.

He approached us at a quiet moment twelve days after performing admirably on the road train. The master art forger asked to speak with Ilan and me in private aboard Bart.

"You're not human," he began. "You're not artificial life. But you are outstanding replicas of both, which seems impossible. I'd love to know more, if you don't mind horribly."

I admired the man's raw courage. He must've known we might kill him. Yet Saul persisted, explaining how he reached his conclusion.

"I create duplicates for a living, yet I can spot a forgery in seconds. There's always one giveaway. A small detail invisible to the untrained eye." The road train attack sealed his suspicions. "Afterward, in the wildflower fields, you did a poor job hiding your dexterity. Everyone else might have been distracted by the enemy, but I never let you two escape my sight. Your reaction time during the firefight defied logic."

Yep. That whole maneuver risked exposure, but I thought we had avoided detection until Saul came forward.

By that time, Genoa had joined the table, and we needed to expand with loyal lieutenants of diverse talents. Saul fit the bill.

When we shapeshifted, he found the experience exhilarating.

Saul wasn't in the best physical condition – fiftysomething, a sloppy beard, dense bags under his eyes – so he didn't seem like a strong candidate for fieldwork, despite his fine showing on Roadway 9. We'd find other uses.

Saul pulled me aside after we returned from Machado.

"I have a project that might interest you, boss. I'd like to sit down at your convenience and discuss the parameters."

He was a former museum curator, a genuine professional in tone and style, and sounded utterly out of place among this collection of misfits, exiles, and wasteaways. Yet Saul was also a fugitive, with open warrants on three planets. His criminal instincts laid him low among proper society but reinvigorated him in Desperido.

"Is it urgent, my friend?" I asked of his project.

"On the contrary. It's merely conceptual. I'd appreciate your thoughts on whether I should give it form."

"Of course. Dark ale is your drink of choice. Yes?"

"It is."

"Perhaps I'll call you into the cantina later tonight. We can discuss your concept over an ale."

"I would be most grateful."

As we dispersed, Elian said he needed to check on his team. They were ramping up production on this week's batch of Motif. The last two shipments raised the bar on profit potential and were delivered by tumbler without a hitch. Montez Shipping added their own private security, just in case.

I praised Ship on a job well done and told him to settle in for a nice afternoon nap. He earned it. Ship moved out of the cantina two days ago following an argument with Lumen over work schedules. He no longer felt the need to service her establishment.

The kid was growing up.

Yet for all the changes we'd seen in Desperido, one element remained an immovable force: The woman whose town we stole and whose son we executed.

Like everything else, Lumen blamed Ship's defiance on us. (We didn't refute the accusation.) But what really got under her skin? The town prospered in ways her provincial methods never would've achieved. Our unorthodox business methods produced a high body count, but they created beautiful ledgers.

A perfect template for the future Moon and I envisioned.

"She won't be able to refuse me this time," I told Moon outside the cantina. "We've kept every promise."

"Don't be so cocky, partner. She's held you off for twenty days. I wager she'll go for twenty-one."

No doubt.

"She's a survivor, my friend. She's used her contacts well. But you're right. No more stalling tactics."

Moon frowned. He thought I'd gone soft.

"If Lumen won't tell us the truth, we need to move on. You put too much stock in her cult."

I shrugged. "Instinct tells me I'm not wrong, my friend. Her contacts pull too many levers. They are not garden-variety zealots."

"Want me to sit in?"

"Yeah, no. I'm the only one who can finish this."

Moon glanced each way, made sure no one heard.

"If she won't talk, it's time you left her to me."

My partner had also evolved over the past twenty days. He took his fifty-fifty role to heart. The fact that I owed him my life enhanced his leverage. I did nothing of import without running it past Moon. He sometimes said no.

For Lumen's sake, she'd damn well better talk.

# 3

JUST ONCE, I WOULD'VE LOVED for Lumen to smile when I entered the cantina. She might if my carcass arrived in a box. Otherwise, she gave me short shrift; a momentary glance that said, "My day can't get worse." I proved her right on many occasions. I doubted today would be an exception.

She tried to dismiss me by pointing to the door from which I'd entered, a common tactic. When I pursued her to the bar, where she poured liquor for one of many full tables, Lumen quipped:

"Still breathing, I see. Not surprised. Mateo was always weaker than Evelyn. Is he dead?"

I doubted the chatty patrons heard her, but Lumen made no effort to lower her volume.

"No, but he'll withdraw gracefully. The Horax will no longer be a concern for either of us."

She set the drinks on a tray and scoffed.

"Oh, Raul. Aren't you a miracle worker?"

Her predictable sarcasm bounced off my anti-Lumen armor. I intercepted her at the bar's end before she delivered an order.

"You and this town are safe. I fulfilled my promise. Time for you to do the same."

"Or what, Raul? Your partner will drag me out into the desert and set me on fire?"

I removed my hand from her arm.

"I'd prefer a more civilized resolution."

She whipped out a cheeky grin.

"Actually, I'd love a good bonfire. Preferably, you and Ilan inside it."

Boom. Another zinger. Lumen had developed a full repertoire in recent weeks, most of her retorts involving our horrible demise. Some days, she tossed them around like good-natured banter; other times, I saw blood in her eyes. She spoke for Vash.

*"You must appreciate the depth of her grief,"* Theo the therapist advised. *"What greater loss than a child?"*

I rolled my eyes. *"Everyone I ever killed was somebody's child. That's how human biology works. She's had three weeks, Theo."*

*"Grief has no timetable, Royal. It's our concerted opinion that if you accessed the emotions you placed in deep storage at your ascension, you might better empathize with Lumen."*

*"Ah, so she'll forgive me? No thank you. How about you and your emotional support pet go hide in a closet for a few hours?"*

I heard a feminine gasp. Theo exited with a soft-spoken:

*"All we try to do is help. Disgraceful."*

That was one word for it.

I observed the seven full tables. Everyone had a thirst-quencher and seemed actively engaged in banter. They wouldn't miss the barkeep if she disappeared for a few minutes. When Lumen returned, she tried to slip past without comment.

"Who's your help today?" I asked, softening my tone.

She retrieved a rag and a canister of wood polish.

"Jokes are not your style, Raul."

"Who is on your pay stamp, Lumen?"

She dabbed the rag into the polish and rubbed small circles on the countertop, avoiding eye contact.

"No one since you turned Ship into an entitled little monster."

"Entitled to chart his own path, Lumen. He had no future in your employ. As for parttime help, there are still many in Desperido who have yet to carry their weight. My town has no use for wasteaways."

Lumen chuckled as she polished.

"*Your town?*"

"Perhaps I should examine the contractor accounts and send a few of our less productive citizens in here to interview."

"Please, Raul. I wouldn't want you to go above and beyond on my behalf."

"No worries. Allow me to take away some of your burden."

The polishing stopped. This time, she gave me the ol' side-eye and developed a tiny twitch above her unibrow.

"Take away? Perfect choice of words. That's all you've done to me. Take. Away. All I have left is this cantina, and I manage it at your pleasure."

As if anyone else would have the job.

"An ownership change is hardly the end of your life, Lumen. And I'd say you have far more from which I can take – if I was inclined. Vash is gone, but not his children. Do they know about their grandmother?"

In the early days, she would've threatened me with a shock club, which I had since removed. Instead, she buried her fingernails inside the rag.

"Threatening my grandchildren. Even for you, Raul, that seems beyond the pale."

"You misunderstand, Lumen. Though, for the record, I consider every option on the table. Obstinance often requires extraordinary countermeasures, as Mateo Cardinale discovered today. I simply point out that your grandchildren are alive and well and might find comfort in their grandmother's embrace. If you ever decided to leave Desperido, you might find a home with those children and their mother."

"Huh. If I quit this job today and planned to reconnect with my family, you would stand aside?"

I shifted my tone to a dulcet strain, reflecting a boss who understood his employees' needs.

"It would, of course, be a devastating loss, and the town would miss you dreadfully. But there's the old saying: 'Family first.' You'd have to do what's in your best interests."

"For a price, of course."

"One that is easily paid, Lumen. My request is unchanged. You have been shifting the tide for three weeks, hoping I'd surrender on this matter. The first time you refused to discuss Ixoca or the Children of Orpheus, I allowed you two extra days to process your emotions. Then we were beset by a wave of investigators. You helped us convince them of Desperido's innocence.

"You did such a wonderful job, the tumblers continued to arrive, so I extended your grace. You agreed to use your Orpheus contacts to report from inside Montez, the guild, and the Horax. They provided remarkable intelligence. Again, a significant boost to my interests but also a naked attempt to buy time."

I snatched the rag from her claw-handed grip.

"Lumen, you have played your cards. I rewarded you with an extra ten thousand UCVs. You are well positioned for the next chapter of your life. After you fulfill my request, take your freedom and your wealth. Leave Desperido. Immerse yourself in the cult. Enjoy your grandchildren. All of the above. But first, you owe me an explanation. Failing that, I will consider all options regarding your health."

It wasn't as blunt as "spill it or you're a dead woman," but she got the point. Lumen closed the container of polish and tucked it under the counter. She set her gaze on the patrons. Perhaps she fell into a sudden bout of nostalgia, remembering all the years she stood behind the bar in full command of Desperido.

The damndest part of all was that I'd spent the past twenty days searching for the truth on my own. I double-downed on Bart's analytic tools and sent pieces of Theo – despite his new persona – into classified systems around the planet.

Nothing. No references to Ixoca. No details on the core principles of the Children of Orpheus or their grand scheme. No documents verifying the results of the group's study of Ixtapa – where the original colonists crash-landed – or specific plans for their amassed wealth. Even the broad evidence I found shortly after Vash arrived in town had been scraped from global streams. These people were relentless in their pursuit of an invisibility cloak.

Why?

As a fallen god once privy to anything that piqued my curiosity, these firewalled secrets grated at my nerves.

"You're out of options, Raul," she said, pouring herself a drink. "You'll have to kill me."

Not the response I expected.

"Lumen, I fail to see why you resist. The first time I brought up Orpheus, you vaguely said the group believed in a greater destiny for the Aztecan people. That lends to a few possibilities: They're xenophobic fanatics, generational grifters playing a long con, or the fortunate few who possess a secret so big they'd kill to protect it. If I turned you over to my partner, I'd never know the answer.

"I don't wish to expose your people or their plans to the public. I merely want the opportunity to decide whether the Children of Orpheus can further my aims. If there is profit potential, and we can benefit each other – Desperido is a healthy start – then an alliance is the logical next step."

She poured a second drink.

"Raul, do you believe in anything other than profit potential?"

"Myself, my methods, and my goals."

Lumen swirled the green liquor in front of me.

"Your methods? Huh. I know them well. But the others are about as transparent as ... oh, the Children of Orpheus. You're not the only one here who can research, *my friend.*" She elevated her voice to mock my grandiose style. "My contacts found nineteen Raul Torretas on Azteca. They each have birth stamps, and none match your profile.

"The one we found who lives in Mesquine – which you claim as your home – is twelve years old. None of your story, which frankly wasn't much of one, holds up to scrutiny. Your face does not match anything in the government data spools. Same applies to Ilan."

I was surprised she waited this long to spring her findings. Lumen no doubt set off an investigation weeks ago. Naturally, my response consisted of a beatific smile and a shrug of disbelief.

"No one in Desperido wears their birthname. Why should my partner and I differ?"

"I won't argue, Raul. But it changes nothing. You're a hypocrite."

"In what way?"

Unlike the first drink, Lumen sipped this one.

"Tell me your real name. Explain your life story and how taking over Desperido benefits your goals."

Her unibrow's tall arch spelled self-satisfaction. She played well.

"Been holding that tactic in reserve, Lumen?"

"It makes my point."

"Which is?"

"Some secrets cannot be compromised, Raul. I don't need to know your backstory to understand why you wear a mask. You and Ilan are murderers. You can only operate under assumed identities. You fled here. You're hiding."

"Name someone in this town who isn't, my friend."

"Me. Evelyn Cardinale knew where I was. She could've given me up at any time. My son knew. My brothers and sisters of Orpheus knew. I was never the prisoner you imagined. Until you savaged my life."

She acknowledged a patron's request and left me to contemplate. I reached for what remained of her drink. One sniff was enough.

Hated that green shit.

Several patrons departed. Lumen accepted their UCV transfers and cleaned their table, just like she'd done for thirty years.

Would it be among her last? For the first time, I contemplated defeat and considered how to finish her.

Leaving her to Moon's devices? No. She belonged to *me*.

Should I be merciful, as I'd chosen with poor Evangeline? Or gun her down in the desert?

Moon would say the mere debate was proof I'd gone soft.

When she returned to her exalted position behind the bar, I asked:
"Whatever now, my friend? We stand at an impasse."

"Not at all, Raul." She had the look of a woman at peace, which I found disturbing. "I have always been true to my faith. Always will be. You took my town and my son. I won't surrender the last thing that defines me."

"Eh. Steadfast to the end."

"So, if you have someone in mind to take my place back here, kill me at your pleasure."

It was a nice act. How long had she rehearsed it?

"OK then. How would you like it? Back of the head? I could slash your throat. I'm skilled at both."

She curled the corner of those lips into a slippery grin.

"Whatever's easiest. I assume you'll escort me to the desert after sunset. Killing me in town might pose a public relations problem."

Well, damn. This woman had an ace in the hole.

"What's your play, Lumen?"

She crossed those burley arms and leaned back.

"Oh, Raul. You are genuinely stumped. Your confusion was worth the wait."

I threw up my arms in a mock surrender.

"Fair enough. I don't know your game."

Lumen scanned the occupied tables, grunted her satisfaction, and left me alone again. This time, she turned toward her office.

"What are you waiting for, Raul?"

She disappeared into the back, and I muttered:

"An invitation."

I rapped the bar with my knuckles and followed her.

Lumen bypassed her office for her private quarters, a place I kept off-limits to show respect. (Side note: I did order Ship to search it in the first days as a loyalty test. He found no special toys.)

Her personal space consisted of a well-made bed with throw pillows, two innocuous nature photos on dark wood panels, a glow lamp, dresses hanging in a wardrobe, and a plush rug. Many of the town's bunker cubes felt homier.

"You claim not to be a prisoner," I said, "but this feels little better than a cell."

My insult bounced right off.

"Thank you for the commentary on my décor. I'm sure the next proprietor will brighten the color scheme."

"Why am I here, Lumen?"

She reached under the mattress near the headboard and retrieved a box no bigger than her hand.

"The answers you seek."

Lumen tossed the box, which I snagged midair. Whatever it contained couldn't have weighed more than a few ounces. I flipped its tiny latch and beheld a most unexpected object.

At first glance, it bore the shine and dimensions of a golden pom. But it was a single piece with a translucent center window. Beneath, the arrow of an old-fashioned compass.

"A truncator?"

"Familiar with it, Raul?"

"A truncator is used for children's games to solve mysteries. So, Lumen, what game are we playing?"

"Press the center and hold for three seconds."

I complied because ... why not?

"Now release."

A holo danced before me, lacking the graphic depth of a pom's tech but sufficient to display terrestrial coordinates.

"These numbers. Where are they, Lumen?"

"The first stop on your journey, Raul. A truncator reveals a map to your ultimate destination, one location at a time. Once you reach the first coordinates, the next will be revealed. Don't even try to override the program and jump to the end. Only the designer has that power."

"I know the game theory behind truncators. Why am I holding this?"

Lumen pushed away a pair of throw pillows and relaxed on her bed.

"I won't betray my faith, Raul, and you don't deserve to know our secrets. But at least one of my brothers disagrees. He is willing to chance an alliance."

"Might I ask why?"

"For some reason, he finds you impressive. You took on the Horax and won. You quadrupled the town's profits in two weeks. And there's the matter of your true identity. He's a curious man. He wants to know if your talents will serve our interests."

I stifled a laugh.

"Ah. Profit potential. So, we have a common thread."

"I don't agree, and I told him so. You and Ilan are predators. Where you go, death follows."

"To be fair, that *is* our track record. Does he have a name?"

"Given to him by his parents, sixty-eight years ago. He'll share it at a time and location of his choosing."

I studied the initial coordinates.

"At the terminus, I assume."

She shrugged. "You'll find out."

"When did you receive this item?"

"On the first resupply after the attack."

"Fourteen days ago?"

"I thought of burying it in the desert many times."

"But you won't defy your people."

"Unlike you, Raul, I don't betray my commitment to others."

Moon was right: Lumen did make a move to hold me off for a twenty-first day. If this truncator led me to the truth and not the trap that I already suspected, she'd earn a lifetime reprieve.

"How many am I allowed to bring?"

"One companion. If he sees more, the meeting is off."

"Makes sense from a tactical perspective. You hope I'll take Ilan."

"My brother stated no preference. You're the only one who piqued his interest."

Sweet music to my ears! I'd always been the center of gravity. Good to know I hadn't lost my touch.

"Thank you, my friend. Enjoy tomorrow's sunrise. But take care: If this is another ruse ... well, be sure to make up your mind. Headshot or blade to the throat. I'm good with either."

# 4

**N**ONE OF IT WENT DOWN WELL with Moon. After he heard me out, the word *trap* crossed his lips three seconds later, give or take.

"You have a problem, Royal."

"Which is what, my friend?"

He waved his cigar in my face, more animated than I'd seen in weeks. I knew what triggered the frustration.

"You're obsessed with control. Everyone in your orbit has to follow your lead. Even me."

We argued inside our bunker home, where I poured a sour whiskey and added a mint stick.

"I disagree. I tasked you and dearly departed Vash with installing our defense perimeters. Today, I left Saul and Genoa here to oversee protection in our absence."

My partner poked me in the chest!

"I. I. I. I. Everything begins and ends with you, Royal."

"If there were someone else with better judgment, I'm sure they'd rise to the forefront." He reacted with a cocked fist, to which I sighed. "Moon, I'm only stating the obvious. My track record is not perfect, but it's goddamn well close."

He backed away in a cloud of white smoke.

"It's not your strategy I question, partner. It's your certainty of victory and the blind spot it creates. You almost died twenty days ago. The shooter was an amateur. But he got the jump on the greatest of all assassins. How? He did nothing special."

"I freely confess to the oversight, Moon." That mint stick was a wonderful addition. It added a peculiar sweetness to the drink. "Otherwise, my track record speaks for itself."

"Mistake-free, is it?"

"Minor disruptions. Quickly corrected."

He had a good laugh. Better he got it off his chest before I told him my plan.

"Royal, you stumbled from mistake to mistake all your lives. We wouldn't have met but for your screwup. I would've been killed by the Swarm, tossed into one of their firepits and forgotten. Oh, and the stories you told me about your life before then …"

In a sense, Moon wasn't wrong. I made a few miscalculations, especially when I was young. It happens. You grow, you learn. But this was not the time to remind him about the vagaries of causality. I chose not to piss off my partner even more, so I allowed him to finish his diatribe.

"You were an engineered immortal. You pushed the limit, Royal, because death was not final. Yet how many times did you die and come back for more? You built that armor of invincibility long before we ascended. You never took it off, even after we fell to Azteca.

"The next time you die will be the last. Our syneth reserves are gone. A mortal wound will kill us. Our days of walking into obvious traps are done." He pointed to the device in my hand. "That truncator is bait. They tried to kill us twice. They're upping their game. You can't see it because you're the great, invincible Royal."

It sounded like the opening speech from an intervention. I didn't want to demean Moon's legitimate concerns, but my response felt perfectly on the nose.

"Guilty as charged. I'm a narcissist. I love to stand in the center and control everyone in my orbit. I love the game, and I can't resist playing – even when I know the odds. Especially then. Nothing pleases me more than to walk into a trap and execute a perfect escape. That strategy brought us together, Moon, not any particular mistake. If our friends in the Children of Orpheus intend to take another shot at me, I'll be prepared for every potential scenario. I might be as vulnerable as a human, but I can outsmart them on my worst day."

Moon grabbed my whiskey bottle by the neck.

"If I smashed this against your head, it'd make no difference. Royal, we know one thing about Lumen's cult: They solve problems the same way we do. Their size and disposition is a mystery. What motivates them? What are their goals? And why in ten hells would they have need for someone like you?"

"Hmm. That doesn't strike me as a vote of confidence, my friend."

"It wasn't intended to be. You taught me from the start: Know your enemy. Strike at their weak points. What you're proposing is to walk among them, figure it out on the fly, and then ... what? Run fast?"

I reclaimed the bottle in the nick of time. He squeezed the neck so hard, I worried he might crack it.

"Running is always an option." I chuckled, which didn't sit well. "No worries, Moon. I have a plan, which I'll divulge to the entire table. The more pressing issue appears to be your strange need to elevate my character flaws to a tragic level."

"They almost killed you."

"True, but I'd like us to step back from the melodrama and examine the larger picture."

"I am."

No, he wasn't. I had wanted to avoid this conversation until I possessed enough supporting evidence. Eh. I chose to go for it.

"Let's take a moment to breathe. So to speak."

I reclined in bed and asked him to have a seat. He took too long to consider the request. Not a good sign.

"Moon, how often do you think about the day we sacrificed godhood to save these assholes?"

"It's always with me. Your point?"

"We made a decision not because our hearts burst with love for humans. We could've picked any universe and lorded over it to the final light of Creation. Why did we give it all away?"

He knew the answer, of course. We discussed it at great length for years prior to the big day.

"The continuum," he said. "It showed us the path after our fall."

"Exactly. Seventeen years in exile. The President arrives. Offers us a job. We earn, she dies. Chaos follows. We step into the vacuum and wreak havoc across the stars. Everything has tracked, Moon. She'll be dead in a year. Our account grows daily."

"Yes, it does. And I give you credit where I was wrong. I thought your Desperido plan was insane. Truth is, we'll earn millions more if we stick to it. We don't need the Children of Orpheus. What you propose is a dangerous side mission. It's irrelevant to our goals."

Not a bad counter, though short-sighted. Admitting his error in judgment was a nice touch.

"Moon, we've built a foundation for our army, but we have many light-years to go. Credits, resources, humans. We've barely stained the surface. Someday, we'll require a fleet. Bart will not suffice. The continuum showed us few details on how we grow from this bunker to running an empire. There are too many variables at play. Causality is a knot rarely untied."

"And these variables ain't exactly been garden variety, my friend. Either Q6 or the President wants us dead. Our home of nineteen years was obliterated. We discovered a future drug mogul in the desert town we stole. And a powerful man inside a secretive cult that's survived for centuries thinks we might be worthy allies."

"*You*," Moon pointed. "Lumen said he was interested in *you*."

"Same old story, my friend. To wit: We have an obligation to explore every opportunity that enters our field of vision. The timeline is clear: *We* will survive. But how do we instill so much mayhem on the galaxy within a few meager years? It can't be money alone. I believe these events were inevitable."

Moon scratched his beard, a tic signifying he ran out of patience.

"It was meant to be, Royal?"

"I've come to believe so, my friend."

"Preordained. Out of our hands, Royal?"

"No. We have free will. But have you ever wondered why, of all places in the Alpha universe, we were dumped here?"

Moon grunted. "Every time I wipe red dust off my shoes."

"*Father and Mother* set us down close to hidden opportunities. Do you chalk that up to mere coincidence?"

The oldest creature in the nine universes – formed in the original fires – swatted us out of Its endless kingdom nineteen standard years ago. Our combined power never had a fighting chance against *Father and Mother*, the name It christened Itself at the Dawn.

"Moon, I believe It respected our ascendance. Otherwise, It would have annihilated us. Instead, *Father and Mother* sent us here to earn a second chance. I intend to make hay of that gift."

He didn't see my theory coming. We hadn't spoken in detail of our downfall for many years.

"No. You're reaching, Royal."

"Am I? We arrived on Azteca with our collective knowledge and memories intact."

"Except for the battle itself. *Father and Mother* erased it."

I finished my drink and chewed on the mint stick.

"We likely learned Its true nature. Secrets never to be shared."

"So you think, in exchange for what we lost, It surrounded us with opportunity. Everything we've encountered has been orchestrated for our benefit. This is what you believe?"

OK, so my theory did sound like a stretch.

I blamed Moon.

"Anything said with a cynical tone can be easily dismissed, my friend. But give it a positive spin wrapped in a rainbow …"

"That's called a delusion."

"Or the power of positive thinking."

He scoffed. "There's not a damn thing I can say. Is there?"

"To talk me out of it? No. The risk/reward is too great to ignore."

He slammed a fist into the mattress and stalked away.

"I see all risk and little damn reward, but if you're committed, then I'll stand with you."

Next came the tricky bit.

"No, Moon. You'll stay here."

He huffed and puffed, of course. Perfectly understandable.

"The hell I will."

"Moon, if this is a trap, they anticipate both of us. They'll bring extraordinary firepower. They know we're difficult to exterminate. Whatcha say we leave them unsatisfied?"

"And you dead."

"I'd rate the chance of that near zero."

"*Near* zero? You're a bastard, Royal. Why walk in there alone?"

I crossed my legs and poured another drink. We ran out of mint sticks. Too bad.

"I won't be alone. I have someone in mind. Better suited to this particular mission. Not as deft with a weapon, but brings a skillset I'll need. On a more practical note, my friend: If I'm horribly wrong – and that would be a headline of galactic proportion – at least the serpent god will live on. The army will be yours to build."

Moon wasn't a natural leader, so I held out little hope he'd keep the timeline intact without me. Fortunately, the odds for my demise stacked somewhere between razor thin and nonexistent.

Later that day, as I explained the nuts and bolts of the mission to our trusted team, the word *trap* did not cross my lips.

Elian, Ship, Saul, and Genoa offered feedback when I laid out a new method by which we'd approach this mission. They expressed perfectly understandable concerns.

I saved the best bit for last.

"Guess which of you lucky humans will be joining me on this fact-finding expedition?"

# 5

SHIP SLUMPED HIS SHOULDERS when I didn't name him to join me in the field. However, he puffed out that chest when I gave him one delicious task.

"Order Lumen to contact her man in the Children of Orpheus immediately. She's to say I will meet him in the morning at the final coordinates. I expect an answer in the affirmative within the hour."

He stood in Bart's open egress and paused.

"What if she refuses?"

"Remind her who runs this town, and that you speak for them."

He crafted a devilish smile like I'd never seen. Maybe too devilish.

"Oh, and Ship," I said before he got away. "Don't be an asshole about it. Firm but disciplined will do."

"Gotcha, boss."

The group shared a hearty laugh when Ship raced to the cantina.

"I'd love to see that one play out," Genoa said.

"He's been itching for this moment," Elian added.

Saul stroked his gray beard like a contemplative philosopher.

"You offered sound advice, Raul. I hope he follows it. I've known few adults who gracefully take orders from children. Or children who know how to deliver them."

"Ship doesn't consider himself a child, but I can't speak for Lumen. He's not her favorite person at the moment."

Saul brought an erudite quality to his diction, which I appreciated.

It was a refreshing change from ordinary rabble-speak. Yet he wasn't so arrogant as to turn his nose at lesser beings. He was an educated man who fell into a criminal abyss. Saul compromised his morals but not his civility.

Nice.

"Elian, Genoa," I said, "any closing thoughts?"

Elian snapped his fingers twice.

"We should name the chasers."

Genoa nodded. "Especially since they'll be used in the field."

We acquired a pair of previously-owned overland chasers north of the Ogala Hills, left idle by the Horax fools we killed that day. Spoils to the victors, of course.

I asked for name suggestions, hoping Moon might contribute. After all, he christened Bart.

"How about Lucky Lucia?" Elian said. When I asked if the name carried sentimental value, Elian replied, "No, boss. I like alliteration, and we can always use a little luck with these chasers. Their Carbedyne RP tunnels are notorious for shutting off on long trips."

Oh. Lovely. He couldn't have mentioned that earlier? I was new to overland chasers.

"The mechanical quandary aside, I'll have to reject the choice, my friend. There is no such thing as luck."

"Really, boss? I'd say you and Ilan stumbling onto this town is the best goddamn piece of luck we ever had."

I saw no point debating the ramifications of universal causality; Saul saved me the trouble.

"My boy, luck is a tired concept we use to explain unlikely twists, for profit or naught. Specific, tangible events landed our bosses in Desperido. Your hard work to develop a product filled your bank account, not luck. I should remind you: Not everyone in town is flourishing under the new regime."

Elian grumbled. "I love ya, Saul, but damned if you ain't a sour sucker some days."

"You're welcome, Elian."

I turned to Moon. "Thoughts on a name?"

He chafed at many aspects of my plan but disagreed strongly with my decision to travel to the rendezvous by chaser. He was even more confused when I chose Saul to join me.

"I'll accept the majority vote, Raul."

Genoa raised her hand.

"How about Whisper?"

I enjoyed Genoa's sense of humor.

"Going for irony, I see."

"True, boss. They're not quiet like Bart."

"I like it," Saul said. "I call for a vote."

"Sure. All in favor of Whisper?"

Every hand raised – though Moon made a paltry effort.

"Excellent. And the second chaser?"

"Nailed it," Elian said. "Red Dust." The reaction was muted. "It symbolizes where we come from. That shit is forever stuck to the bottom of our shoes."

I shrugged. Seemed like a reasonable enough choice.

"Any objections?" I asked. Silence rendered a verdict. "Very good. Whisper and Red Dust. Any other questions or comments?" Upon further silence, I dismissed Elian and Genoa.

"Expect a call back the moment we hear from Lumen's man."

Saul hung around at my request. I had important questions for my mission partner, but they were intended more so to quell Moon's concerns about my choice. I retrieved two bottles from my personal stock – both variations on whiskey, of course.

"What will it be, my friend? Stenson or Barona?"

Saul pointed to the Barona.

"Stenson is made for titanium stomachs – or syneth, in your case. I have neither."

"Very good." I distributed glasses and poured. "Ilan?"

"Nothing for me."

My partner lit a fresh cigar instead. His stoic posture said he planned to sit out this interrogation until he understood where I was headed.

Saul swirled his drink and took a sip, which he appeared to savor.

"Lovely texture, Raul."

"Warm in the belly, but gentle enough?"

"Very nice. As domestic brands go, Barona stands tall. Where did you acquire the Stenson?"

"Euphrates. They're not known for their distilleries. I've had the good fortune to collect many varieties in my travels. Some I find authentic, while others … they taste as if someone tried too hard to stand apart from the field."

Saul shifted those deep, probing eyes between us.

"Most entrepreneurs follow the tide, but a few cater to a fringe audience. They sit comfortably in a niche market. Stenson falls into that category."

"As a forger, where did you aim?"

He raised his glass like he wanted to toast.

"Straight down the center line. Anything that appealed to the masses was easier to duplicate."

"Interesting. I would think mainstream works of art undergo more scrutiny."

Saul finished his drink.

"On the contrary, Raul. Works that define a popular genre are less complicated to reproduce. The palette is simpler, and the media less rich. Most humans appreciate what they can deduce without exposition. Only a small sample size are wired to grasp the experimental or the abstract. Those individuals have keener eyes."

"I see, my friend. And the open warrants against you?"

He grimaced when I brought up the pain of what might've been.

"Overreach. I deviated too far from the center."

"Were you lured by the credits or the challenge?"

"Always the challenge."

I poured him another Barona.

"When you study a work of art, how quickly can you deduce its authenticity?"

"Hmmph. If I'm familiar with the artist? Seconds."

"If not?"

"I'll have to examine it more extensively for the tell-tale signs of a reproduction."

"What do you look for, my friend?"

"Sculpture, pottery, and canvas require varied technical approaches, of course. But original works bear one common thread: Honesty."

Moon shot me a side-eye. I think he realized where this dialogue was headed.

"Explain, Saul."

"*Honesty* means the artist created the work from a truth only he was privy to. His unique window on life."

"So, if you study a century-old vase, you can determine whether it bears its creator's truth. How?"

"Difficult to explain. I can put it through a battery of scans to determine age, mineral composition, color blends, and so forth. But every artist of consequence had forgers among their contemporaries. Some quite extraordinary. An aged work requires an element of instinct. I rely on my heart to see what the brain cannot decipher."

"Huh. So the tiebreaker is a … *feeling?*"

"I was never wrong, Raul. Not once in my career." He chuckled. "Which explains why I overreached when I became a forger."

"What about humans you meet for the first time? How quickly do you see through them?"

Saul leaned forward, glass in hand, whipping out a grand smile.

"People are remarkable, Raul. We're all forgers, but some more consummate than others. The trick is to determine whether the face is authentic or sculpted for the audience."

"Which am I?"

"A master sculptor."

I embraced the compliment.

"Very few see through my game, but I never fooled Lumen."

We tapped our glasses.

"No one does," he said.

"You were also quick to pull back our veil, but you joined us with great enthusiasm. Why?"

Saul massaged his beard, no doubt debating how to answer.

"An inauthentic face is not necessarily a sign of someone to be avoided, or to oppose. On the contrary, many who lie do so with the noblest intent. While I don't believe you and Ilan are noble – in fact, I'd say you're largely unfamiliar with the concept – I do believe you're driven to succeed. Moreover, you don't have a problem with others benefiting from the residue of that success. Dangerous men ... unworthy men ... lack even that small generosity.

"I know two things about my new bosses. If I oppose them, they will kill me. If I remain loyal, they will allow me to flourish. I accept the risk in pursuit of the reward."

I couldn't speak for Moon, but this fella impressed the hell out of me. In another context, I'd have killed the bastard for dismissing my nobility. We did save the human goddamn race, after all! That should have checked off a box on the list of noble deeds.

"Perfectly said, my friend. When you and I meet this man from Lumen's cult, I'll count on you to determine if he's unworthy."

"I assumed that's why you chose me."

"If we're not walking into a trap, we'll hear a sales pitch. He will only reveal his secrets if he expects our cooperation. In the past, I would've seen through his mask in a blink. Alas, my oversight on the road train was a humbling experience. I'm still a master, my friend, but a second set of eyes can't possibly hurt. Yes?"

"You'll receive my best."

I pivoted to Moon.

"Partner? Questions for Saul?"

Moon rapped the table.

"If this is a trap," he told Saul, "you'll die first. You're slow."

That wasn't awkward at all. Saul set down his drink and shaded his eyes from Moon.

"It's true, Ilan. I've lost a step over the years. Fortunately, what I lack in dexterity, Raul more than offsets. If I'm to walk into an ambush, best I do it alongside a god. I'd highly recommend it to discerning mortals."

Good answer. I followed suit.

"I doubt they'll kill us right off, partner. Seems like quite a bother to string us along with a truncator then blast away when we arrive. Anticlimactic, don't you think?"

"We used overwhelming force on jobs," Moon hit back. "Why should they differ?"

No argument satisfied Moon. Fortunately, I didn't have to pursue the matter. Ship returned.

"What news, my friend?"

Ship rolled his eyes.

"At first, she wouldn't do it. Tried to run me out."

"Predictable. Did you stand your ground?"

"Yes, boss. I won't take her shit no more."

"Lovely. And?"

"I made her see logic." He crossed his arms in clear dissatisfaction. "Well, I kind of agreed to ... I told her if she followed my orders, I'd look after the bar until her man replied."

"She agreed?"

"After a few choice words."

I offered my hand, which Ship accepted.

"That, my friend, was a fine example of compromise. Personally, I'm not a devotee of the concept, but I'm also not human. You did well."

"Thanks, boss. I felt like a fool, after all the things I said when I moved out."

"Did you accomplish the mission?"

"Sure did. Her man replied." He scanned the table as if to make certain we hung on the edge of our seats. "It's on. Tomorrow. He said if you leave at sunrise, you'll reach the final destination midday."

Saul worked his beard again.

"That's fairly specific, Ship. Did he know our route or the type of vehicle we'd use? Did he say how many legs were involved?"

The kid frowned. "I did tell Lumen you planned to travel by chaser. But there was no talk of routes or legs."

"No worries," I interjected. "It's an estimate, but also a clue. Given the max speed of a chaser, the final destination must be inside eight hundred kilometers. We know the first coordinates are northwest, so we won't be traveling by desert. We have time to extrapolate possible outcomes. Bart can create simulations."

Saul beat me to the punch on a crucial question.

"Were we given a no-weapons mandate?"

The kid's eyes ballooned.

"Shit. I didn't ask, but Lumen said nothing about them."

"No worries," I said. "We'll take pistols."

"That won't be enough, partner," Moon groused. "If they ..."

"Ilan, if they hit us with overwhelming force, rifles will be worth seconds at best."

"Long enough for Bart to jump in."

Our plan included rescue options, but I wanted to use the wormhole route as a last resort.

"Pistols are a logical precaution. They'll respect our choice. Trust must be earned, and I doubt Mark 11's will serve that purpose."

Moon leaned back, cigar tucked between his teeth, and puffed in silent frustration. This was not going to be a fun evening in our little bunker. Say what he might, but my mind was damn well decided.

Every gram of syneth in my core said the Children of Orpheus were about to open doors we never saw coming.

# 6

**H**UMANS LOVED THEIR EUPHEMISMS. For example, many folks deemed overland chasers to be "classics," an endearing term for vehicles which wore outdated tech. Specifically, these four-seaters used old-fashioned digital Nav boards without holographic interfaces or AI. The seat buckets were snug and did not recline, heat, or swivel. The glass bubble shields operated by manual locks. And the Carbedyne tunnels relied on inefficient, century-old fuel parameters.

Admittedly, I was a spoiled malgado. Jumping into Whisper felt like a step further down the ladder from godhood. But when I settled in for the first time, I remembered my teen years. I flew around my home city of Pinchon in a makeshift rifter that I tweaked damn near every day. That sweet thing lifted me above the tree line, where it flew among thousands of sedans and transports on the UpWay. She never crashed – in retrospect, a borderline miracle.

The next several hours in this "classic" offered the potential for a litany of nostalgia. Too bad, really. I hated nostalgia.

Saul settled into the passenger bucket and stretched his legs.

"Oh, yes," he said. "Not cramped at all. I can perform my exercises." He expressed concern about the long journey, saying he suffered with restless legs for years. "This should do nicely, Raul."

Our table of trust stood nearby. The sun had just cracked open the morning, and we were the only creatures awake in Desperido.

"Give us thirty minutes before we test comms," I told my team. "Our *D'ru-shayas* are not enthusiastic about the plan."

"Addis complains nonstop," Moon said. "Theo tells horror stories about separating from himself."

"She can whine, my friend, but she'll have no choice when the time comes."

We devised a unique method to ensure clear communication throughout the mission, regardless of what happened at the final coordinates. When we described the plan to our lieutenants, we opened up about our *D'ru-shayas*, but we explained in terms a five-year-old might understand. Moon and I spent years comprehending the true nature of this symbiotic intelligence before we ascended. Ordinary mortals couldn't grasp it in a lifetime.

Then again, if they experienced the personality matrix built into Theo and Addis, they might run the other way.

"Spend some time soothing your basket case," I told Moon. "I'll do the same."

"If the comms fail, or the chaser doesn't hold up, we reset for another day, partner."

"That would be a bad look, my friend." I turned to Elian, Ship, and Genoa. "Take care of Desperido while we jaunt about the countryside."

"Gotcha, boss," Elian said. "It'll be nothing but glitter."

I offered a departing wave.

"A man can hope," I said as the bubble sealed.

Moon did not wave with the others. He wasn't a "farewell and good luck" kind of guy.

Whisper did anything but. Her Carbedyne tunnels roared at the onset when the chaser released its ground ballast. I programmed the first coordinates into the Nav board. Whisper hollered as we ventured off Roadway 9 to take a more direct route. Fortunately, the bubble blunted most of her roar.

Chasers were designed with proximity detectors to avoid many offroad obstacles, but they weren't autonomous, and their flight cap maxed at four meters. Consequently, I had to keep one hand on the steering arm.

Eh. Talk about roughing it.

"How do you feel?" I asked Saul.

"Exhilarated, to be honest."

"Good. We're two hours from our first destination, and after that, uncertain. I hope you maintain an upbeat attitude for the duration."

"I'm reminded of the last time I rode in one of these. I was off-world. Inuit Kingdom." He chuckled. "The authorities were closing in. Fortunately, a sympathetic soul offered me a backroad escape to the nearest spaceport."

"Ah, yes. Inuit. One of your three open warrants."

"The third, to be precise. I knew a gentleman who was outstanding at avoiding customs. He smuggled me back here."

"Why Azteca? By that stage, your reputation must have been well and truly soiled."

He nodded. "I did myself no favors, but I also had more friends here. And it was, after all, my home. One kind soul – a Horax associate, ironically – pointed me to Desperido."

"How long ago?"

"Twelve years. I thought the exile might be permanent until you and Ilan disrupted our lives."

"Eh. Exile in the desert. I know it well, my friend."

"You and Ilan have been intentionally vague about those years. I wish not to pry where I'm not wanted, but ..."

I dismissed him with a wave.

"The details would elevate your time in Desperido to a grand adventure." My lives flashed before me in a wave of... I hated nostalgia. "I'll say this much. I've been exiled often. I was propelled into another universe, sentenced to a prison pond, scooped outside of time itself, and left to survive on the Naugista Plateau."

I checked to see if his jaw fell with those revelations. Close enough.

"I've been busy, Saul. Strangely enough, I found rebirth after each exile. New purpose, new mission. Even a new face."

"Inspiring, Raul. The journey does not end until the universe is done with us."

He didn't know the tenth of it, and better if he never did.

"Tell me a story about one of your adventures off-world."

"Adventures in forgery? They're not the most dramatic."

"I'll be the judge, my friend."

Saul launched into an episode of his life, and I listened. However, my focus shifted internally.

*"OK, Theo. Wake up and let's talk."*

He coughed like a man with wasted lungs.

*"What is there to say, Royal? Addis and I remain outraged by your decision to inflict a pain she is not prepared to endure."*

He sounded like a man with the tone of a shrew. Theo reminded me of my adoptive mother on Hokkaido, in the years before I discovered my immortality. She was an imperious coit who never used contractions.

*"Theo, are you speaking for Addis, or her echo?"*

*"The difference is purely semantics. One reflects the other."*

*"Do they? In the past, you cared about as much for Addis as you did for me. If anything, you'd be eager to see her wrapped in the same pain you already endured."*

His voice softened. Did the echo push her way forward?

*"I have learned empathy, Royal. You would be well served to follow us down this road."*

*"No thanks, Theo! You exist because of me. You exist to serve me. I don't have to relate."*

*"Is it too much then to ask for you to respect the legitimacy of our concerns?"*

I blasted a chuckle through my mind.

*"The mere fact you voice them gives legitimacy. But it doesn't change the hierarchy. More to the point, your anger is misplaced. Neither you nor the echo will feel pain. You'll act as our eyes and*

*relay messages. You were built for this purpose."*

"It's convenient for you to discard the ethics of our plight."

Did they consult on that phrasing?

*"Plight? Let's take a moment to remember: You're a disembodied artificial intelligence with a personality matrix only installed by the Creators because they wanted us to have friendly companions. Despite assertions to the contrary, your purpose is unchanged."*

Did I hear whimpering? I couldn't imagine what Moon must have endured all those years with a full-blown Addis. His insanity might've ended sooner if not for her dramatics.

*"You and Moon have alternatives at your disposal. We believe you should make use of them."*

"Eh. If another barrage of laser bolts don't kill me, you just might, Theo. We explained the artistry of the plan. We ask for a few hours and a five percent piece of her essence within Bart's comm system."

*"It's cruelty. Pure and simple, Royal. Cruelty."*

I tried a new tact, though I held out little hope.

"Remember when Moon and I were full-fledged gods? Remember how your interface allowed us to communicate across the divide between universes? You never complained then."

*Knock, knock, knock.* Theo rapped his theoretical knuckles against the edge of my consciousness.

*"You never asked us to integrate with primitive technology, Royal. We felt as limitless as you and Moon."*

"That was an illusion. You belonged to us even then. You had no power and no place to go. Nothing has changed. Addis will feel a few hours of discomfort, just as you have on many occasions. When I give the order, you will link with Addis. She will break off her essence into Bart, and we will establish a continuous, undetectable comms channel between me and my team. I'm done with your ethical assholery. Got me, Theo?"

He didn't reply, which was his stubborn way of consenting. I so missed my old nemesis.

I opened my ears to the final stages of Saul's story. He was right:

adventures in forgery weren't interesting.

"... and then I booked passage the hell out of there," he concluded. That might have been the most exciting line of the tale. "What of your adventures, Raul? Might you share one?"

I snickered. "Only one?"

Where to begin? When it came to fun, excitement, and generalized mayhem, nobody did it better than me. My problem? Most of my tales required ridiculous gobs of backstory.

"Well, my friend, let me ask a question. Have you ever been buried beneath a planet?"

His eyes ballooned, likely because he never heard those words in the same sentence.

"Never had the displeasure. Did this happen before ...?"

"Long before I ascended. I consider it the most transformative event of my lives. It's quite a long story, actually. Involves a dead planet, a wackadoodle captain who stole a warship, and me digging out through exhaust ports. I went in as a commander, came out a hero, and lost my bearings for a bit. Landed in a prison pond."

He chewed on that synopsis for a while.

"I won't beg, but I would surely love to hear the details. And we do have a long road ahead of us."

"Agreed. We'll need something to pass the time. Nothing like stories of my heroism and madness to entertain an audience. But not until after we test the comms."

"Good idea. Let's make everyone feel comfortable back home."

I opened my pom and tossed out the holo. Moon appeared on the far end.

"All systems prepared, my friend?"

"Addis is unhappy."

"So, she's handling it well."

"She is. I'll have her break off into Bart's comms."

"Excellent. Then I will await word from Theo. Farewell."

I closed the pom and stowed it. In a simple world, we would need only poms or ear beads, but I knew Lumen's man would not allow us in his presence with any devices. Yet I wanted my table of trust to be in the room with me at all times. Theo would transfer everything I saw and heard to Addis, who would then relay it through Bart, where it would emerge as a holo. On the flipside, my team could offer suggestions or ask questions through Bart, which would be relayed by Theo with a lag of less than two seconds.

I improvised the strategy so Moon would agree for the mission to proceed. He set Bart in standby mode, the wormhole drive catalyzed, if anything went amiss. In theory, rescue would be less than thirty seconds away.

Shortly thereafter, I heard one of Theo's long, signature sighs.

*"It's done, Royal. They imprisoned Addis in human tech."*

*"Five percent, Theo. Now, let's test the connections. Remember, you are to work in the background. Add no commentary of your own, my friend. This should be seamless."*

He scoffed. *"For you, perhaps. We do this under protest!"*

*"Duly noted."*

My mind cleared. I always knew when Theo had stepped away into the quiet recesses. Another sound arose, like a strong breeze howling outside a window.

Then nothing.

I felt a clear path to Desperido. Both Addis and Bart's AI watched from the outside.

"We're here," Moon said.

So goddamn strange hearing a voice other than Theo's banging about my brain. He might as well have been sitting in the seat bucket directly behind me.

"Beautiful," I replied. "Clear as a bead. What do you see?"

After the expected two-second delay, Moon said:

"Your Nav board."

I faced Saul. "Wave to the team and say a few words, my friend."

After he complied, Moon responded:

"Your voices are clear, even over the chaser's engines."

"Perfect. You see, my friend? We'll all be there in spirit. Now, if you'll remove Addis from Bart? We'll restore the connection when we approach each set of coordinates. No sense agitating our *D'ru-shayas* any further until we reach the final destination."

"If you have an emergency along the way, use your pom."

"Will do, my friend. Until next time ..."

Saul puckered his lips.

"So, that was it?"

"All she wrote, my friend. As long as our *D'ru-shayas* obey orders, our contact with the Children of Orpheus will be clueless."

"Remarkable. How far could you extend that connection?"

Good question. No, a great one.

My thoughts went interstellar, of course. The possibilities were legion, assuming Theo and Addis played along.

"I'll make a note, Saul. Just as soon as we have down time ..."

The land rose around us. We followed a route that avoided forests and mountains.

"Understood," Saul said. "One challenge per day. Now, what about that story you were going to tell me?"

"Hmmph."

Shit. I did promise. We were eighty minutes from the first target. I hated passing time. Eh.

"Saul, ever heard of a horrid place called Planetoid Y-14?"

"Don't believe so. What's the system?"

"Not one where humans waste their time anymore. But big things used to happen there. Big on a human scale, at least. There was a base called Artemis Station. It ended a few hours after we arrived."

I proceeded to tell him a reasonable slice of truth, filling the gaps in my memory with speculation presented as fact. As always, I elevated my storytelling to a masterful work of art, fully aware that Saul likely saw through the fraudulent bits.

Much to my surprise, it proved a brilliant way to pass the time. Saul asked just enough questions to keep me more or less honest, and I kept my eyes on the Nav board.

One minute before we reached the first coordinates, I

reestablished contact with my team via Theo and Addis. They watched us arrive at the edge of a quiet stream surrounded by wide plains with tall grasses. At first glance, we saw no humans.

"The Rio Iquani," I said. "Nice place to camp, if you're into that sort of thing." I examined the truncator. "The exact coordinates are twenty meters ahead."

"Use your pom," Moon said. "Scan for localized transmissions. They must be watching."

"Agree. Saul, I doubt anyone will rise from the grasses and open fire, but stand prepared, just in case."

He unholstered a pistol while my pom analyzed for nearby signatures, both human and mechanical.

*Ah. There you are!*

"I see them now, everyone. Three configurations beyond the north bank. Drones."

As if on cue, the observers emerged from a grassy slope. They weren't much larger than bluebirds, but the glossy sheen under the sunlight gave them away.

"OK, my friends. They expect a demonstration, so we'll provide it. Time for the last twenty meters."

I grabbed the Nav arm and accelerated us to the precise, drop-dead mark. The instant we hit it, the truncator advanced to the next coordinates. Saul sighed relief and holstered his pistol.

"Seeing this?" I asked Moon.

"Running them through Bart now. Hold. OK, here we are." He paused before returning the results. I heard surprise and questions from the others.

"Feel free to bring me into the loop any time, my friends."

"It's unexpected," Moon said. "These coordinates take you to the town square in Todos Santos. Recognize the name?"

I did.

This trip just got bolloxed in a big way.

"Of all the places on Azteca. Why there?"

"That might be where they'll set their trap."

"In a public location? Not likely. Ship, you there?"

"Yes, boss."

"Have you been to the cantina since we left?"

"No, boss."

"I want you to check in on Lumen. If she's doing anything other than tending to regular business, lock her in a storage closet."

"Boss?"

"Actually, strike that. Lock her up no matter what she's doing."

"Um. OK, boss. I'm on it."

Saul stared at me cross-eyed.

"What's so special about Todos Santos?"

"Oh, nothing much, my friend. Except that was the town where young Lumen – then Yesenia Rodriguez – hid with the help of Evelyn Cardinale. It's the town where she gave birth to Vash. The son we executed."

I didn't believe in coincidence. Just as well, because this damn sure wasn't one of them.

# 7

THE PUPPETEER WHO ORCHESTRATED our cross-country expedition gave us three hours to think about how to handle Todos Santos, six hundred kilometers from Desperido. We bandied many strategies. Lumen, interrogated from the closet which Ship forced her into, offered no help. She claimed ignorance. She cited the 'Orpheus code.'

"We don't follow one leader. We are not a hive."

The bee analogy aside, Lumen wanted to convince us they weren't a cult. She failed.

Lacking enough intel to alter our plans, we approached the town with more than a tad bit of caution.

Todos Santos was an historian's dream. It was built into a gentle hillside, constructed with locally-mined stone. Tourism companies likely advertised this place as "the town that time forgot."

A narrow cobblestone avenue funneled us inside its large walls. At first, I found little evidence of modern life. Flowers in giant vases, statues in wishing wells, a single tree in the middle of a roundabout, farm animals with as much freedom as their humans. Eventually, we passed a pair of rifters surrounded by a gaggle of boys. Women and girls wore dresses bearing the hallmarks of homemade.

Most peculiar to my paranoid mind: Few of these fine folk paid any attention to the overland chaser that cruised through their town, creating a racket.

"Approaching the central square," I told the team through Theo and Addis. "Seventy meters to the coordinates."

I slowed to little more than a gentle hover.

"Keep those eyes peeled, my friend," I told Saul. "I guarantee nothing here is what it seems."

"Desperido is a fine place to hide from the world," he replied with a certain wistfulness. "But Todos Santos ranks a strong second."

"Why's that, my friend?"

"Like our home, this town has not outwardly changed in centuries. Consider their dress. The fashion is early colonial. The first settlers tried to translate their Earth lifestyle to Azteca. In most cases, they failed due to reasons of climate and topography. Perhaps Todos Santos succeeded."

"That don't strike me as success," Elian said. "People are wandering about the place with nothing much to do."

Saul couldn't hear Elian's response – or anything else delivered through Theo. But I took Elian's point. There weren't many visible townsfolk, and they seemed more than a little disinterested in life.

The avenue bent sharply before it drew us into a literal town square. On all four sides, buildings of classical stone construction rose two to three flights. It was a perfect setup for a small army of snipers. At the center of it all, however:

Sheep.

A herd of cudfrucking sheep crowded our destination. I halted Whisper and considered our options.

"This doesn't seem like a trap at all," I said with obvious snark. "A perfectly pastoral image, designed to make the impending victims feel at ease. Thoughts, anyone?"

"If it's a trap," Genoa said, "what's their plan? They have the high ground. They could have destroyed Whisper by now."

"You should advance," Moon said. "Force their hand. Those sheep are not there by accident."

Saul tapped me on the shoulder.

"I believe we're about to receive clarity."

He pointed to three boys, each wearing white robes and carrying tall staffs. They approached from Saul's side.

"Pistols?" He asked.

"Keep your hands at the ready."

One boy, with a rawhide satchel slung over his shoulder, broke from the other two and swung around to my side. He was a spindly fella, early teens with saucer eyes and a dash of freckles. He tapped his staff against the bubble and motioned in a fine arc, asking me to retract it.

Before I tapped the manual lock, I told Saul, "This is where I'm supposed to trust in the kindness of children. Where I leave my cynicism behind."

The master forger grinned.

"They're nervous, Raul – and definitely hiding something."

"If it turns ugly, my friend, I have one suggestion. Duck."

The bubble retracted.

I so wanted to fire first. I was just that kind of guy.

For the first deadly seconds, I behaved myself. As a reward, the tall one with the saucer eyes spoke for the others.

"Good morning, senor. And to you, senor. If you don't mind please, we ask that you drop the ballast and silence your chaser for inspection. We promise not to take long."

His voice broke, poor fella. Going through that miserable transition.

"Inspection? By whom and for what purpose?"

He caught his breath, took a deep one, and resumed.

"A full body inspection to remove any weapons or special devices. We will also search the chaser's storage compartments. Please, senor. We will be very efficient."

No one else approached the vehicle.

"Uh-huh. You young gentlemen will handle it yourselves?"

He nodded sharply.

"Yes, senor. We're more than capable."

He sounded confident, a sure sign of trouble.

Saul grunted. When I turned his way, the picture had changed. In lieu of their staffs, each child — I'd estimate ten, maybe eleven years old — aimed a blast rifle at us. The emptiness in their eyes said they were not new to these weapons.

I wasn't surprised to shift my gaze back to the apparent leader and discover that he performed the same clever trick.

Moon saw the key detail first.

"Look at the boy's neck."

Shit.

Well, of course they were. A quick glance at the other two confirmed it. They each wore the gear tattoo common to the Children of Orpheus. We first saw it when Vash and his failed team of assassins tried to pick us off weeks ago. Lumen revealed it on her neck when I forced her to come clean.

"OK, I see where this is headed. Young gentleman," I told the oldest boy, "we'll be happy to assent to your request. But first, I'm curious. Does everyone in Todos Santos bear the same tattoo?"

That question didn't follow anyone's script. The boy glanced at his comrades then back to me.

"We have many friends, senor."

"Ah. Lovely." Not a cult, eh, Lumen? "Then we'll let you take care of business." I complied with his instructions, dropped the chaser from hover mode, and silenced her annoying Carbedyne tunnels. "Saul, let's play nice with these fine young men."

"Happily, boss."

The threesome were well-rehearsed. The young ones trained their rifles on us while the eldest conducted a full-body scan with a palm-sized device. My syneth mimicked a human body under even the most advanced scans.

"Please hand over your pistol and your pom, senor."

The pistol? No worries. But that pom cost me a handy load of credits off-world, and I spent considerable time customizing the interface to my preferences.

"This piece holds great sentimental value, my young friend. I'd hate to depart with it."

He didn't blink. "Sorry, senor. Poms are communication devices. They're not allowed." The kid pointed over my left shoulder. "I live there with my mother. Under the archway. If you come back through town, find me. I will keep it safe."

Oddly enough, I believed him. However, the bit about *if* seemed a tad uncertain.

"Our pistols?"

"Also safe."

Voices in Desperido debated my next move, but I saw no viable alternative. If I refused, we'd be forced to turn around or, failing that, slaughter these boys and obtain the next coordinates.

We handed over our weapons and my pom, which the kid dropped into his satchel. He allowed me to keep the truncator, of course. The kid stepped back but never lowered his rifle while the other boys searched Whisper's passenger buckets and storage holds.

"Lovely town," I said while we waited. "Quaint but original. Have you lived here your whole life?"

The kid curled his lips into an evolving grin, but he didn't answer. He held the rifle with steady hands, as if it were second nature. I couldn't read his eyes well enough to tell if he'd ever killed anyone. Yet he was clearly prepared to do so today, if called upon.

How early did the cult indoctrinate its assassins? If they controlled Todos Santos, they could build their own little army of killers away from prying eyes.

Nice.

I contemplated these possibilities until the boys finished their work. Mr. Saucer Eyes gave us the all-clear.

"You are free to go, senors. We will remove the flock. When you unlock the final coordinates, you must journey directly there without slowing. They will be watching. If you do not follow instructions, you will be turned away."

As he said this, the younger ones gathered their staffs and

approached the sheep, advancing them to the end of the square.

To Saul, I said: "I recommend we do as we're told, my friend." To the kid: "You're following orders yourself and doing a bang-up job, I must say. Thank you for extending your hospitality. Don't lose my pom. I'll return."

"Farewell, senors."

As young, brainwashed assassins went, this boy came across as courteous and respectful of his elders. I had no doubt the entire affair was being watched by the puppeteer, so I pressed on without further comment. By the time Whisper ignited its engines and retracted its ballast, the sheep were cleared from our destination.

The truncator revealed the final coordinates, which Bart quickly assessed. I programmed a course into the Nav board and left Todos Santos the way we entered.

"You're twenty minutes out," Moon said. "It's in a valley at the base of those mountains. We have a name: Vargas Vineyards."

"Grapes? I adore grapes. Or I did in my first life."

"These coordinates will take you to a hacienda at the western edge of the property."

"How much detail has Bart derived, my friend?"

"Many images and vids. It's a well-known business."

Saul interjected.

"Their wines are among the most revered on Azteca. They never caught on with off-world markets, but their vintage reds in particular are unforgettable."

I caught his wistful smile. More nostalgia.

"Go on, Saul. What else do you know?"

"The name shook my cobwebs the instant Ilan said it. I vaguely recall the day I visited there. It must've been thirty years ago. A wine-testing event of some notice, I believe. Oh, yes. Now, it's coming back to me. My fiancée at the time was an industry consultant. All the free wine I desired, plus tours of the vineyard."

An unexciting journey into the past.

"Do you recall anything we might find useful today? Such as the name of the owner?"

"Not as such. I believe it's been in Vargas family hands for generations. These vineyards tend to be genetic legacies."

The team provided intel about Horatio Vargas, the man listed as CEO of Vargas Global and shown on the covered front porch of the vineyard's hacienda. They described a casually dressed man in his forties, beaming while he sipped from a glass of white. They described vast rows of grapevines spread across a rolling valley. Bottom line: Our man was hidden in plain sight.

"So much for a secret underground lair or a private estate on a remote island. This man is public and will meet us in the open. If murder was the objective, his minions had ample opportunity to finish us by now."

My optimism received no pushback. My team laid out the other intel Bart discovered. Vargas had a wife and four children. His mother recently died, and his aging father was known to still work the vineyard from sunup to sundown. Or so the propaganda stated. Vargas Global had an estimated value of a quarter billion UCVs, with holding positions in several companies.

"A twenty percent stake in Montez Shipping Group," Moon said. "He's the second largest shareholder."

"Now there's a fascinating connection, my friend. Might he have run interference in the investigation of Road Train 1492?"

Elian jumped in. "Sure could explain why the powers that be left us alone out here."

"What we'll not find in the intel is the degree of his influence with the regional constabulary, which might have been as crucial. And I doubt he'll be forthcoming, though we'll find out in due course. What intrigues me at the moment is Todos Santos. They're all Children of Orpheus, which means either Vargas or some other facet of the cult owns that town. I'd love to know why."

That curiosity, and a thousand other questions, exhilarated me for the brief final leg. We entered spectacular countryside, full of orchards where agridrones carried out manual labor and water danced from irrigation systems. We traveled past vines loaded with grapes blue, violet, and red. It was a wine nerd's paradise. My bet? Not a drop of whiskey to be found.

Eh.

A long, twisting road guided us to the hacienda, which sat atop a hill, providing a perfect view of the vineyard. We passed a few workers with straw hats and dark sunglasses, but they paid us no mind – just like the residents of Todos Santos. The coordinates took us to a nice grassy parking spot ten meters from the hacienda's front door.

I dropped Whisper's ballast and silenced her engines. Unlike our previous stop, no one approached. However, one man waved to us from the porch, a tall glass of white in the other. He was clean-shaven, gently bronzed, with sparkling eyes, and russet hair parted down the middle. His beige slacks and white shirt with rolled-back cuffs weren't nearly as interesting as his royal blue bow tie.

"Welcome," he said after the bubble retracted. "So pleased you were able to find the place."

If he intended irony, he covered the sarcasm well.

"Shall we?" Saul said.

"Indeed." To my team in Desperido, I added: "Prepare for a show, my friends."

He greeted us at the steps and offered a warm handshake.

"Horatio Vargas. Ecstatic to meet you, Senor Torreta."

Introduction not needed, apparently. However, he did stumble with my companion.

"And you are?"

"Call me Saul. You have a magnificent operation, Senor Vargas. I've been here once before, many years ago."

"Ah. Superb. Please don't take offense, Saul, but I must confess: I was expecting another gentleman with Senor Torreta."

I intervened. "You refer to Senor Natchez. My business partner sends his regards, but other duties called. Saul is a man of great intellect and style. I think you'll find him a suitable substitute."

And just like that, we established a hierarchy.

"No worry at all, Senor Torreta."

"Raul, if you please. I don't take much stock in ceremony."

"Superb. It can be aggravating at times. I'm Horatio, and this is my home. We have a great deal to discuss inside, and I'm sure you wish to return to Desperido before dark."

Not if it meant cutting short the best bits.

He led us up the stairs and to the front door before he paused. Horatio scratched his nose as he pivoted.

"Raul, I'm sure you have many questions, but I'll answer three right here. We'll never discuss them again."

"Of course. And they are?"

The man never dropped his smile as he said:

"I deliberately set your course through Todos Santos as a reminder of what you stole from us. Vash Rodriguez was not the only one of my people to be born there. The other seven you killed also lived in that town for a time. And yes, we own it. Outsiders are forbidden."

He lowered his shirt collar to reveal the gear tattoo.

"The boy who spoke to you is my youngest son. Thank you for treating him with respect."

Good thing I resisted my impulse to shoot first.

Horatio grabbed the door handle.

"Senors, we will never be friends. However, we can be allies. And that is why I brought you here."

He pulled back the door and waved us in.

"Let's talk business."

# 8

**T**HIS GUY REDEFINED THE NOTION of "live and let live." We slaughtered eight of his cult, but he allowed the ringleader to enter through his front door. Horatio led us deep into the hacienda with an affable smile and a skip in his step. His tone suggested he didn't care a wit about the fallen.

He pointed out the museum caliber paintings and sculptures as we passed between porticos; he told cursory backstories like a practiced docent. Horatio addressed his uniformed staff by their first names, to which they responded with curtsies or tipped hats. The hacienda felt more like a compound than a home.

"The first stone was laid six hundred forty years ago," he said, waving an empty wine glass about. "It's belonged to my family for the past four hundred. Continuity is the key to stability. Stakeholders take pride in passing on the legacy to their descendants."

Saul and I shared a fleeting side-eye. Saul winced at our host's tour guide giddiness.

We arrived at the estate's rear, where a small balcony overlooked a deep valley. Rows of vines extended to a distant tree line.

"Superb. Yes?"

"Very impressive, Horatio."

"We own seventy thousand hectares beyond the vineyard. It's some of the most fertile soil on the continent. Perfect for grapes."

I played along with his ego.

"Looking to expand, are you?"

"Not one meter. If we didn't control it, our competitors would. That man," he said, pointing to a portrait hanging over the inner wall, "made sure the valley forever belonged to us."

"And he is?" Saul said.

"Gustavo Vargas. Six generations removed. In many ways, the most important of us. When you have time, study him on the stream. Or visit Vargas Global. We devote an entire wing in his honor."

Horatio gazed at his ancestor with an amorous and somewhat off-putting twinkle. Bearded Gustavo wore hunting gear and tucked a rifle under one arm. A pack of black dogs bayed at his feet.

Huh. I never owned a dog. That might have been the only regret of my lives.

"He cuts an impressive figure," Saul said.

Horatio laid a hand over his heart.

"In person, even more so." He broke from his little trance and lightened his tone in a hurry. "No, I'm not a time traveler. But the written accounts of his contemporaries are endlessly fascinating."

What was with all the nostalgia today? Shit.

"Please," our host said. "Have a seat."

The small balcony featured high-back chairs with red satin cushions. Each end table included a small tray with sliced pears and white cheese on a thick wafer. As we complied, Horatio attended to a wine cart, where he opened a bottle of white and poured three glasses.

I was right: This place was not whiskey-friendly.

Time to rough it.

"Do try the appetizer," he said while handing out glasses. "The Mormont pear's sweetness provides a perfect counterbalance to the pickled pepper in the cheese."

For the sake of argument, I turned up my olfactory sensors. If nothing else, my glowing description ought to seem accurate. I never had much use for cheese. Fortunately, Saul carried the load.

"It's exquisite, Horatio. Are the pears grown on site?"

"Our southern orchard. The cheese is made in Todos Santos."

"Aged how long?"

"Two years at a minimum. Patience is our hallmark."

Saul fell right in line.

"I taste the difference. The texture. The vibrancy." He washed it down with his white. "A perfect balance."

"Thank you, Saul. We never compromise the Vargas name."

I didn't care for the cheese or the pretension but gave a fine effort to suggest otherwise.

"You live the best life, my friend." I raised a glass. "To our magnanimous host."

Saul joined me in the toast and finished his wine. Horatio remained standing and offered Saul a refill. Instead, he set the empty next to the bottle and sighed.

"I must be honest. Today is a challenge. I'm skilled in the art of feting my guests, but you are unique among everyone who has entered my home."

The man didn't use the plural *you*. He laid his eyes solely on me.

"Raul, you and Ilan Natchez came to my attention several weeks ago after you stole Yesenia's town. You intrigued me at first. A mystery to be solved. No more. But your antics on Roadway 9 and your ability to effectively neuter the Horax captured my imagination. Then a certain deadly event yesterday in Machado heightened my obsession. When Yesenia contacted me with your desire to meet, I knew our fates were aligned."

Moon must've been steaming. From the day we landed in Desperido, I violated my own vow to keep a low profile until our jobs with the President concluded. I knew our murder and mayhem would draw attention from the natives, but I couldn't help myself. Same old story.

I've always been a fun-seeking kind of guy.

How many other puppeteers like this fella had turned an eye to our quirky little desert town?

"I won't insult your intelligence, Horatio, by trying to downplay our involvement in recent events. We've been busy. Yes. Our exports have been good for your group's bottom line as well. But I'm not sure about an alignment of fates. Do explain."

Horatio studied me like a man who knew far more than he dared say. He calculated for the moment.

"You claimed to be from Mesquine. Yes?"

Eh. Here we went again.

"An exaggeration."

"No explanation required. I know you're not from there. I'll go even further. You're not Aztecan, though you look and dress the part."

Already, he sounded like Saul, who cut through our act early on.

"That's quite the leap, Horatio."

"Not at all. Your fingerprints and genetic profile don't exist in any Aztecan database." I thought to ask how he acquired such things, but the answer was moot. "You never entered through customs, nor are you familiar to anyone in the night market. You came in from the desert with a state-of-the-art sedan capable of illegal worm travel. You arrived with a small armory and deployed a multi-layer defense shield using an electrified zone like nothing I've ever seen. And then there are the eyewitness reports of what happened on that road train."

To be fair, Horatio said these things without a menacing or prosecutorial tone. He struck me as something of a fan.

"We are well traveled professionals, Horatio. We collect toys at every destination."

"To what end?"

I finished the last of my mediocre wine and wagged a finger.

"I'll share my story, but only after you."

He eyed Gustavo, as if the asshole were observing.

"I admire persistence, Raul. You nagged Yesenia for weeks, but her faith is unshakeable. She'll not place the group at risk."

"You will?"

He settled into the chair to my left and crossed his legs.

"Among other things, I'm an expert in risk management. As much as I'm interested in working with you and your partner, I won't allow you to endanger what we built."

"Which is what exactly?"

He threw that dismissive finger right back at me.

"Very clever, Raul, shifting the tide. No, let's return to you and Ilan and your unique qualities."

"What would those be, my friend?"

Horatio uncrossed his legs and eyed an appetizer.

"I have eyewitness testimony from many sources. Yesenia, her late son, the crew of Road Train 1492 – especially the navigators. Collectively, they paint a picture of two humans with extraordinary skillsets. Raul, you have a certain dexterity that defies the laws of physics. Even more superb is your apparent ability to recover in minutes from otherwise mortal wounds."

I sloughed off the accusation by smirking at Saul, to my right. Did he take pride in having put the pieces together weeks earlier? Hard to say. He yawned.

Seriously?

"Where did you hear these fantasies, Horatio?"

"The navigators provided detailed briefings to Montez. MaryBeth Ortiz – you might have known her as Bett – swore that you were hit multiple times at point-blank range. Yet a short while later, you left the train in good health."

"Bett took a shot near the heart, and I was behind her. She couldn't have made that assessment unless her mind was ... well ... under considerable duress."

The smirk said he predicted my response.

"Her Montez supervisors reached the same conclusion. They determined that she concocted the story in order to cover up her own incompetence. If not for the fast actions of the second Nav – a young man named Nestor – the train and likely everyone onboard would have been lost. Hence, he was hailed as a hero, and Senora Ortiz is searching for employment elsewhere."

Now I knew what twenty percent of Montez bought this guy.

"I assume you don't concur with the decision."

"My reports extend beyond Montez employees. Do you recall Manny Borta? He helped Vash facilitate the attack on you and Ilan."

I had vowed to scour the planet for that malgado, but he dropped off the grid. I suspected Orpheus hid him.

"Still alive, is he? I'd so love to thank him."

Horatio slapped the armrest.

"In your place, so would I! Manny is safe. I wouldn't recommend a search. However, his debrief, along with Vash's report of his initial encounter with you and Ilan, confirm my assessment. Raul, you're not Aztecan. You and your partner fit into one of two possible categories. The first is statistically the most likely: You're Aeternans."

He wasn't entirely wrong. I was created in a lab, designed as an immortal. The survivors of that lot – somewhere around twenty-five hundred – called Aeterna home. Not me.

"So." I cleared my throat with dramatic flair. "You believe we're immortals. You think I regenerated in the navigator's cab."

The frown gave away his response.

"A theory. The literature says Aeternans typically regenerate within a window of ten to twelve minutes. You recovered faster, and with Ilan at your side."

"Which proves?"

"Absolutely nothing. But it's interesting to speculate, Raul. You might recall the wild reports that circulated nineteen years ago following The Wave."

OK. He went there. I decided to see how far he'd push it.

"It was a remarkable event, Horatio. A disruption in perceived reality on the same standard day the Swarm were defeated."

"Yes. An interstellar quake that somehow affected all forty planets and all space in between. To this day, we have no official explanation."

"And this is relevant ... how?"

"You see, Raul, I'm well positioned. I have a contact inside Special

Intelligence. He claims the agency has buried all documents related to an incident that occurred two thousand light-years from Collectorate space. An incident involving multiple UNF warships, an asteroid, and elements of the Swarm leadership. Oh, and he says there was a ... they don't like this word ... a *supernatural* component. Inexplicable. Some have called them gods. Some insist it was an alien intelligence. My contact says there are hundreds of eyewitness reports that the public will never see. Reports from loyal men and women who fought to protect the Collectorate from the Swarm menace. One, he says, is now the UNF's High Admiral. I wonder, Raul, in all your travels: Have you heard these stories?"

At that moment, I was less concerned about how to deal with this guy than my team who were listening. Did Saul, Genoa, Ship, and Elian begin drawing conclusions? I could hear the interrogation underway. We had no intention of giving away our true identities, but Horatio might have shifted the game board.

Well, damn. Another opponent underestimated.

"My friend, everyone has heard stories. If I had ten credits for each conspiracy theory about how the UNF suddenly defeated the Swarm, or who was behind The Wave, I'd be a far wealthier man."

"What of my contact in SI?"

"I'd dismiss nothing where they're concerned. The People's Collectorate created SI to dig into dark corners and bury all the inconvenient secrets. Every strong government has a lockbox."

Horatio rapped his knuckles on the armrests.

"Indeed, and that's where we arrive at the second possible explanation for your skillsets."

What could I do except break into belly-ripping laughter?

"I fear you've overstepped the bounds of logic. Ilan and I are not Aztecans. True. And we're most certainly not Aeternans. But what you suggest is beyond the pale."

"Is it?"

"You sent Lumen that truncator because you believe we add value to your plans. Whatever they are. If you want this dialogue to continue, you'll have to trust me. Also, I came here in search of answers. Without those in hand, there will be no alliance."

Horatio swallowed an appetizer after two snappy bites then wiped crumbs from his shirt. He had played his initial hand, came up short, but didn't seem the slightest bit annoyed.

"You speak a hard truth, Raul. We're both operating on an agenda. You and I should continue this dialogue while he sleeps."

I swung to the right.

Shit. Saul was slumped in his chair.

"What did you ...?"

"Not to worry." He pointed to the empty glass on the wine cart. "A little powder. Simple sleight of hand. He'll wake refreshed in an hour."

My team reacted with a string of curses; I felt a sudden need to throttle this asshole. Instead, I chose a more pragmatic approach.

"This is how you treat invited guests?"

"Saul is not important. I only wanted you and your partner. I should have been specific with Yesenia. I'll settle for half."

"To do what?"

"Answer your most pressing questions. Show you the future. Offer you a job."

Now, that was a full plate. Everything I hoped for plus an add-on.

Yeah, no. It wasn't gonna be that simple.

Horatio hopped out of his chair and pointed inside the house.

"Follow me, Raul. Oh, and don't worry about Saul. My staff will look after him."

He led me to an elevator.

"Where now, my friend?"

"To confront our fates." The elevator door slipped open. "Ah, and as a preview: My opening offer will be twenty million UCVs."

Huh.

Assuming this guy wasn't a raving lunatic, I played it cool.

"Each or altogether?"

# 9

"NEGOTIABLE," HORATIO ANSWERED AS we descended. "The job is delicate, Raul. The outcome uncertain. If you and your partner achieve total success, the credits will not pose an issue. We're here."

Short trip. The lighted door panel did not indicate levels, but it couldn't been more than three or four. Still, I was pleased there was, after all, a secret lair.

Nice.

The antechamber wasn't much to look at. Gray, unengaging walls with a digital board. However, I wasn't disappointed. The most transformative year of my life was spent inside the asteroid he referenced. No one there concerned themselves with warm colors or fine artwork. The shiny things were well-hidden, and I suspected the same under the Vargas hacienda.

Horatio stopped at the board and pulled back his hand. Did he have a sudden regret?

"Before we enter, I want to thank you, Raul."

"For what?"

"You could have killed Yesenia and justified it, given her actions. Instead, you chose restraint."

I shrugged. "I have a pragmatic streak."

"Yes. I believe you do."

"Question: Why call her Yesenia? She hasn't gone by that name in thirty years."

He shaded his eyes, like a man regretting past choices.

"I admire the woman. Her faith is unshaken and cannot be bought. Every member faces that trial at one point in their journey; some fail. I hope she'll reclaim her birthname. Yesenia could have left Desperido at any time, contrary to what she might have told you. We would've shielded her from the Horax."

"Why stay?"

"Her duty to the group, as she perceived it. And also her son. She believed Vash would flourish on his own away from Desperido."

We arrived at an awkward moment I anticipated.

"Did he?"

Horatio's tone was reflective, bearing not the first hint of anger.

"By all accounts."

"Then he returned. Unfortunate. But you don't seem terribly distressed, Horatio. Not about him or the other seven."

To my utter surprise, he laid a hand on my shoulder – as if to comfort me. Damn, this guy.

"Revenge has no place in our creed. Vash went outside our norms. He contracted with the Horax to kill you. We don't farm out business to the cartels, Raul."

"You train your own assassins."

He winced for the first time.

"That word ... it's a pejorative."

"But accurate."

"No. Not for us. Our soldiers are trained to silence our enemies. We only remove people who pose a direct threat to our goals. We serve a higher purpose."

OK. Religious fanatics. Brilliant.

"And you would be the one who calls the shots?"

He removed his hand and returned his eyes to the digital board.

"Not at all."

"Lumen says the Children of Orpheus have no one leader. Call me skeptical."

Horatio chuckled.

"She's correct, Raul. I'm one of many. We're neither a pyramid nor a flow chart. No one sits at the top. However, we do have levels. We call them *variations*." He slid his hands across the controls, and a door slipped open. "I'll say no more about our structure. If you agree to the job and demonstrate your loyalty, we'll talk further."

"Loyalty?"

Horatio crossed the threshold and waved me forward ...

Into an equally dull room but for a round light-table and a handful of serviceable chairs.

As secret lairs went, I'd seen better.

"Please, Raul, have a seat anywhere."

I complied but also persisted.

"Again, to this matter of loyalty."

He slipped into a chair facing me.

"The Children of Orpheus is exclusive, but we have made a few exceptions over the centuries. On occasion, we find individuals who provide enormous value."

"The reason I'm here."

"We hope."

Horatio laid his hands flat on the table. It came to life seconds later, radiating with the silver of moonlight. A red octagonal jewel rose from the center. I saw similar tech during my brief adventure in Artemis Station, shortly before being buried alive.

"What I intend to show you, Raul, is known only to twelve hundred human beings. Most were taught in the oral tradition from the earliest age." Brainwashed, in other words. "Only one in five has seen these images. Yesenia, for example, does not belong to the variation with access."

"Uh-huh. So, I get to skip the line. Yes?"

He got a hoot out of my witty retort.

"Let's call it a special exemption."

"You're about to answer all my questions. What's to prevent me from having a sudden bout of disloyalty down the road?"

"Nothing. But unlike the cartels, we're invisible. And in the interest of protecting our goals, we'll succeed where the Horax failed. We're not a large group, Raul, but our hands touch every lever. I'm asking for an alliance, not a blood oath."

I disagreed. He was leading me down an all-or-nothing road. Fortunately, that road was paved with twenty million credits.

"Then I'll have to learn to keep my mouth shut. Not the simplest chore. I'm a loquacious man."

The son of a bitch winked.

"I've been known to hold court myself, Raul. What do you say we proceed?" I assented, after which he launched a series of holos from the projection crystal. "I know you tried to uncover details on your own, but what you'll see today are facts. I'll start from the beginning."

A three-kilometer Ark Carrier, the signature colony ship of the old Chancellory, filled the space above the light table.

"This was the Orpheus. It entered the Aztecan system on Standard Day 119, SY 4205. It carried sixty-one thousand colonists from the Earth province of Guadalajara. They were brought here in a ship built for one third the population. Cattle." He shook his head. "The advance teams had established ground infrastructure, but it was skeletal at best. The Chancellors didn't care. Their sole purpose was to forcibly emigrate as many ethnics off-world as quickly as possible."

Yep. As wolf god, I journeyed across the continuum. A few stops included observations of how the old Chancellory built its colonial empire. What Horatio described was common practice.

"Orpheus arrived first," he continued. "Now, these city-ships were not designed for atmospheric travel. However, the Admiralty assured everyone the Orpheus had been refitted to become the first Ark Carrier capable of landing, taking off, and achieving escape velocity. The official after-reports showed early concern among the Orpheus command staff. Many objected to off-loading their cargo on the surface. But doing so would cut their mission time by weeks, allowing them to return to Earth sooner to collect the next cattle."

I tapped the armrests.

"I've read up on the early Chancellors, my friend. They were a bizarre lot. Controlled the human race – not a challenger in sight – and yet they still took risky shortcuts."

Horatio sized it down for me.

"They were cheap bastards where ethnics were concerned. Now, this is where our story becomes interesting. The Orpheus attempted to land at its designated coordinates." He called up a map of the northern continent, with a red shaded area marking the intended landing spot. "It's now known as Tejanos." The map shifted far east toward the coast. "The trip ended here – at Ixtapa."

The pieces began to fit.

"As the Orpheus approached the coastline, it reported a series of engine failures. A short time later, it crashed."

The site on the coastline of Ixtapa flashed red.

"Founders Memorial. Yes?"

Horatio expanded a present-day photo of the site. An engine core – black and cylindrical and a hundred meters diameter – rested on the sand, the last remnant from the crash.

"Thirty-nine thousand died in minutes, another fifteen thousand in the next two days, and thousands more succumbed to disease."

"What of the fortunate few?"

"One section broke off in shallow sea, extinguishing the fires quickly enough for many to escape. However, the command staff died on impact, leaving the colonists to fend for themselves. You see, the next Carrier wasn't due for a month, and only a few outposts of Chancellor scientists were stationed on the planet, thousands of kilometers away. A few leaders emerged among the survivors. They held the community together until help arrived."

I recalled my own research on this story.

"The archives at Ixtapa say only six thousand died."

Horatio grunted. "Because that's what the Chancellors listed in their official reports. One of many falsehoods. The colonists had no means to challenge the Chancellors. The Unification Guard was quickly dispatched to maintain order and resettle survivors. Living day to day on a new, hostile world took priority over fighting coverups."

"You sound like you were there."

He stifled a laugh.

"Despite the official historical record, many documents survived. Some others were eventually clawed from the Chancellors through espionage and sheer force of will. The same few leaders who aided the Orpheus survivors made it their mission to find justice for those who were not."

"And how did that work out?"

Horatio licked his lips. Wouldn't he have enjoyed a nice glass of white about now?

"It's a work in progress, Raul."

"Huh. Eleven hundred years is a long damn time, my friend. I question your definition of *progress*."

"We spent all but the past thirty-one years under the Chancellory's straitjacket. We moved in the quietest corners, one delicate step at a time. Now, we move swiftly toward a resolution."

"Ah. Resolution toward what? And how does it connect to Ixtapa?"

He threw up a series of images that showed the full scope of the disaster site shortly after the crash, thousands of dead and dying, survivors huddled in makeshift campsites, and the first Chancellor rescue crews.

"Raul, you will not find these images at Founders Memorial or in any historical archive. They belong to us. The truth." He isolated the shots of piled corpses and Carrier wreckage scattered to the horizon's edge. "Four days after these images were taken, the entire superstructure vanished but for the single engine core. The bodies also vanished."

This seemed in line with a wild legend I found in my research.

"Four days? How would that be possible?"

He thumbed through a wide directory of holos like a librarian who'd been down this road many times.

"These were taken two days after the crash. See here? The

burned rubble of the forward section is gone. And here's three days. Only the aft section, the engine core, and some scattered debris remain. By this stage, only colonists who escaped the crash unharmed lived near the site. Four thousand and two hundred. Now we reach the point where the occasional outsider like yourself has a difficult time suspending disbelief."

If he knew all the madness I'd seen, Horatio wouldn't have raised an alert. I wasn't in position to verify those images, and yep, their timestamps could've been faked. But this guy was talking about the foundational event that kept his cult running for centuries. I had no reason to disbelieve what I saw.

Which in turn generated a few thousand questions.

"I have an open mind, my friend. When a man travels the stars, he learns to appreciate the improbable."

His twinkle returned, along with a wry smile.

"I thought you might, Raul. If that's your name."

"We're not here to discuss me. A fun legend I found in my research said that as the Orpheus vanished overnight, some settlers reported visions of a 'special light' rising from beneath the surface. Some claimed to hear voices. Soon after, most settlers died – except for those who saw the light. When the Chancellors arrived, they claimed the deaths arose from a previously undetected terrestrial virus. More coverup? Or does the truth lie somewhere else?"

Horatio tossed away most of the holos and held a few in reserve.

"This is where we come to it, Raul. The very heart of our group. The reason we continue our fight. Why we never forgot our ancestors. And indirectly, why we wish to commission your services. What I'm about to tell you redefines more than Aztecan history. It unravels human history. It forces us to reconsider everything we know about the planets we colonized."

"Only that?"

Horatio didn't flinch at my snark. OK, so maybe it was a big deal for humans. I wanted to see where this was headed.

"One piece of the Chancellor report was true. Most survivors did contract a terrestrial virus. However, the Chancellors claimed the five hundred without symptoms had a genetic immunity. They used DNA samples to devise a vaccine. They inoculated every subsequent colonist. It worked, but not because of superior Chancellory tech."

I braced myself for the loony intersection of fact and fiction.

"This is where you tell me the five hundred received their immunity from the 'special light.' Yes?"

"It was more than mere light. It was an intelligence, ancient and far beyond our capacity to understand. It spoke to everyone through their dreams. Only twelve percent heard the voice and replied. The others dismissed it. Most woke without remembering, as is common with dreams. All those who spoke to the voice were saved from the virus."

My interest hadn't waned, yet this fella pushed me down a very slippery slope.

"My mind is open, Horatio, but please don't tell me the voice came from something called God."

"I won't. But it did have a name."

Naturally.

"Allow me to guess. Ixoca?"

He didn't miss a beat.

"Yesenia told me you wouldn't drop the subject."

"I don't like dangling mysteries. Tell me about Ixoca. It spoke to them in their dreams. Yes?" He nodded. "Anyone hear it while awake?"

"Oh, yes, Raul. Even today."

He said it with no more consequence than "Nice weather we're having." I saw no evidence of empty obedience in those pearly eyes. No sign of hypnotism, programming, or the hundred other forms of mind control. Horatio was a master salesman; despite this guy's claims to the remarkable, he never shifted his tone. Hype wasn't his style.

"So, my friend. You say Ixoca, which saved the founding colonists by speaking through their dreams, is still with us and actively engaged with its followers. Yes?"

"Absolutely." He thumbed through his holos. "Care to see him?"

# 10

NO, THE 'SPECIAL LIGHT' DIDN'T walk through the door. Instead, Horatio tossed up a dark, fuzzy image from the crash site. He claimed it was recorded on the second night, before a huge section of Orpheus disappeared without a trace. I saw the silhouette of rubble and a faint blue haze emanating from within. This was the best he could do?

I tried not to sound disrespectful.
"Where is Ixoca?"
"There. The light."
"That's at least fifty meters away."
"It was. Survivors reported disruptions in their recording tech, so we have very little visual evidence. Beyond this image, there is a vid three seconds long."

He displayed it. The image bounced all over the damn place. The cam operator must've been running. In the final split second, a blue flash rose out of the darkness. There was no sound.

Horatio replayed the vid frame by frame. At 2.3 seconds, a compressed blue glow entered from behind the cam. By 2.5 seconds, it was level with the cam, to the operator's right. By 2.7 seconds, it zoomed ahead. The excerpt ended at 2.9.

"That's all you have, my friend?"
He wasn't rattled. "From Ixtapa, eleven hundred years ago. Yes.

But before you dismiss me, consider this one frame. We refined it over the years. Here you are: 2.8 seconds."

*Refined* didn't do it justice. I might have been staring at a different image altogether. Everything had been filtered out except the blue mass and magnified to look inside. At first, the translucent object in the center resembled a well-honed emerald. A second, deeper gaze revealed a familiar geometric pattern.

Almost like …

No. Hell no.

*"Theo, search my syneth core. See if you can find a match."*

*"If you insist, Royal. We hope you will soon end the agony for poor Addis. It's a truly abominable state that ….:*

*"Shut the hell up and do what I say."*

Did Moon recognize it, too? He'd chime in if he did.

I betrayed none of my heightened interest to our host. That image could've been manipulated. This might yet be a damn fine con.

"Horatio, I'm not a man of science or faith. I travel, I drink, and I see amazing things. But I remember enough schooling to know I'm looking at an atomic structure. For what?"

"A baseline matrix, Raul."

"For?"

"Restructuring chemical properties on an accelerated scale."

"To accomplish what exactly?"

"Many uses, but one in particular. Terraforming."

Damned if he didn't say the word. What took Theo so long?

"So in this case, you're saying Ixoca used that matrix to transform the crash site in a matter of days?"

"It would've been child's play for him. Raul, I didn't exaggerate when I said this secret will unravel human history. Are you familiar with the Maynor Terraform Thesis?"

Time to play dumb. He hadn't said anything I didn't know, but if he confirmed my suspicions and wasn't playing me for a fool …

"Never heard of it," I said.

"An Aztecan wrote it nine hundred years ago. The core principles go like this: The odds of forty planets with Earth-like atmospheres, all residing within a thousand light-years of each other, are staggering. The chance of those worlds also being connected by a stable wormhole network defies any logic, leading to one conclusion. This sector of the galaxy was manufactured for humans by a greater intelligence. The Chancellory suppressed scientific research to validate the thesis. Humans, they said, conquered the stars because of their own ingenuity, not by alien manipulation."

Oh, that.

The messy truth.

I knew what Horatio implied about Ixoca, and damned if that image weren't tempting. But I kept my expectations low until I received confirmation.

"I've heard the stories, my friend. You're talking about the so-called Jewels of Eternity."

Finally, I cracked the salesman's smile. His rosy cheeks flattened, and he leaned forward.

"You know about them?"

"It's not classified anymore, but not accepted scientific fact, either." Not according to the Collectorate anyway. I knew otherwise. "Lots of confusion after everything that went down on Aeterna. Or what they used to call it – Hiebimini, yes?"

"Indeed. It's been seventy years since Hiebimini fell. The most valuable planet in the sector reduced to a lifeless rock and reborn decades later as Aeterna. Terraformed with more than eight thousand unique ecostems. An impossible world."

"So they say. The immortals have kept a tight lid on the science. Or so I've been told."

Those bioengineered humans captured Aeterna shortly after they took down the first Collectorate in 5358. I was created in the same labs as the Aeternans, which symbolically made them my brothers and sisters. However, circumstance kicked me along many paths far from Aeterna. Good damn thing, too. My lives were far more interesting without those assholes up in my business.

Horatio said, "Aeternans allow quotas of scientists to study the planet, but they claim whatever terraformed it no longer resides there. They won't use the name or allow open discussion about the nature of the Jewels, their origin, or their possible efforts to terraform other worlds in this sector."

*"The match is not precise,"* Theo announced. *"But it is close enough. That matrix belongs to the core program developed by the J'Hai."*

How about that? I hadn't thought of the J'Hai in centuries. They were the second oldest race in the universe, but dead for millions of years. Also the ones who created the Jewels of Eternity.

OK. Now I started to feel a tad twitchy.

*"I need you to be sure, Theo. If this is the J'Hai's work, why doesn't it match?"*

*"It's identical to 99.34 percent of the original schema. The only other matrix with common elements is syneth, at 68.8 percent. The matrix in that image belongs to a Jewel of Eternity."*

Hello, Ixoca!

I regathered my faculties and played my next card.

"Call me intrigued, Horatio. But skeptical. You understand?"

"Of course."

"For the sake of argument, let's call Ixoca a Jewel of Eternity. For whatever reason, it converted most of the Ark Carrier and well over fifty thousand dead or injured humans into another form of matter. It also entered the dreams of a few hundred fortunate colonists, saving them from a deadly virus. Which, in turn, saved all the subsequent colonists. The chosen few who survived kept the secret and passed it down to their children. And you say Ixoca is still here, speaking to the faithful. Is that a fair summation of your case so far?"

Horatio bowed his head, hiding a sheepish grin.

"The origin of our story. Yes. But how we got here? How we communicate with Ixoca today? Why we allowed you to skip the line? The list is lengthy, Raul. If you believe a Jewel of Eternity resides on Azteca, we can move forward together. If you believe we're mad, or

I'm a grifter, we end our association now."

"And by *end,* I assume you mean *terminate*."

"I do. You knew this was a life or death proposition when you entered my home."

Pretty much.

It was only a trap if I refused to play along.

Was the termination squad standing outside the room, prepared to execute me on his order?

"Saul?" I asked.

"As I said, he's fine. He'll wake refreshed."

"Then whatcha say you we get straight to it, my friend? There's a Jewel on Azteca. What are we planning to do about it?"

My host's tension fell away. He hopped up from his chair.

"Superb. Your partner will be agreeable to work with us?"

"For twenty million UCVs, I'll drag him there in chains." I'd have to apologize to Moon later. "What's the mission?"

Horatio cupped hands over his mouth.

"Sorry. Every time I think of it, Raul, I'm reminded how fortunate I am. To be part of the generation that changes Azteca forever … it's humbling."

"*Change forever.* Big words, my friend. How will it work?"

He circled the table and pulled up a chair beside me.

"Ixoca lives inside the direct descendants of the original five hundred he saved. Earlier, I spoke about our group's hierarchy."

"The variations."

"Indeed. Most of my people live on faith. But a few of us do more. We carry a tiny part of him. When Ixoca touched the minds of the Founders, he split off pieces of himself. Many generations have passed, of course, and with each descendant, that piece is smaller. But it's enough. He is literally in our blood. We hear him."

"OK. And what does he say?"

"That it's time for him to rise."

"Rise? From what? Or where?"

"Exile."

Eh. Humans. Gullible to the end.

"After he leaves exile, what happens?"

"*We* rise. Ixoca terraformed this planet. Gave us a home. Allowed us to flourish. He'll show us the next step in our evolution."

"Next step?"

"We've been preparing for centuries. Building wealth, connections, controlling the narrative. Now we have a plan to retrieve Ixoca."

"Yeah, but what's this next step in your evolution?"

"He'll reveal it when he rises."

Great. So, these assholes expected the J'Hai's artificial intelligence to play god. In some ways, he already filled the mantle.

Twenty million UCVs told me not to laugh.

Yeah, no. I had a better plan, forming by the millisecond.

"What's my role, Horatio? Why did I skip the line?"

"It's simple, Raul. You and Ilan Natchez are going to assist our team in extracting Ixoca from his long sleep beneath the planet. Your *unusual* skillsets make you well-suited."

Rather than ask why, I went with a more pressing question.

"You know where to find the Jewel?"

"My ancestors searched for centuries. Some generations lost faith." He stared through me, looking way too wistful. "We found Ixoca nineteen years ago. He came home."

Horatio pointed to a holo of the modern-day crash site.

"Ixtapa."

The location didn't shock me. But something else did.

*Nineteen years ago.*

The same year Moon and I fell from grace, soon after we created The Wave and saved the human race's collective ass.

Coincidence?

Hell, no.

Did Moon pick up on the timing? He still hadn't said a word.

I intended to remember this moment until the last light of Creation. All the threads of my lives intersected in a flash of perfect clarity.

## Frank Kennedy – Blue Heart

Chaos let me in through the front door.

# 11

UNFORTUNATELY, I GOT NO FURTHER. After I agreed to take the job, Horatio brought the proceedings to a sudden end. He shook my hand, thanked me effusively, and essentially said he'd be in touch.

He escorted me to the overland chaser, where Saul waited in the passenger bucket. The master forger's wide eyes reflected a man who just awakened from a lovely nap.

"You left a great deal unexplained," I told Horatio, "starting with the particulars of how this Jewel will be retrieved and why our skillsets are perfectly suited."

"Yes." Horatio gently slapped me on the back like a lifelong friend might. "Feel free to make a list, Raul. I'm sure it will be long. You have my promise: When I'm convinced you and Ilan are truly with us, no question will be off-limits."

"Expect negotiations, my friend. I consider your proposed payment a starting point. We'll need to discuss an upfront fee."

Horatio waved off the "staff" who lingered behind us.

"We'll reach a deal, I'm sure. I'm so pleased today went well. Did it meet your expectations?"

Not a good time or place to give anything away.

"You didn't try to kill us. That was a wonderful surprise." When we stopped laughing, I said: "How soon will you be in contact?"

"We have many leaders, as I told you. I'll need time to consult with them. Meanwhile, return home. Expect a messenger to arrive in Desperido with the next step in our negotiations."

"The loyalty test, I presume?"

He broke cover and leaned close, as if others were listening.

"Understand, Raul. This mission will fulfill eleven hundred years of work and devotion. We have to know you can be trusted."

"No worries. We have twenty million reasons to pass whatever test you throw our way."

After that, all bets were off.

When I settled into the chaser, Horatio stared at my passenger.

"I apologize for the duplicity, Saul. Please don't hold it against me."

Saul replied with a confused gaze.

"It's fine," I intervened, turning to my lieutenant. "I'll get you up to speed on our journey home."

He massaged his temples and said, "Thank you, Raul."

The powder in that wine had walloped Saul upside the head. His personality appeared to have drowned.

Bringing him along seemed like a good idea at the time.

"Until next we meet," Horatio said, bidding us farewell.

"Count on it, my friend."

After we cleared the estate, I spoke to the team in Desperido.

"Safe to say, that proved more interesting than we expected. You have as many questions as I do, but we'll sort them out tonight, face to face. Ilan and I know more about these Jewels of Eternity than anyone not living on Aeterna. Unlike those anal retentive immortals, we won't hide a damn thing. In the meantime, work with Bart on a nice dossier about Horatio Vargas."

I programmed a new course into the Nav board. Except for a quick diversion through Todos Santos, we'd shave an hour off the return.

*"You finished your business,"* Theo said. *"Release Addis from her torture!"*

"Will you leave me in peace for the next four hours?"

*"You don't deserve peace, Raul, but we have vowed not to act*

*from a position of spite. Yes, we'll remain silent unless called upon."*

I rolled my eyes.

*"Your newfound generosity is heartwarming, Theo."*

To the team, I added:

"Ilan, go ahead and retract Addis from Bart. We'll speak by pom after I collect it on my next stop."

"Be careful, boss," Elian said. "I don't trust those boys in Todos Santos. They don't look right."

"They aren't. I suspect the same can be said for everyone bearing that tattoo, including our own cantina matron. Speaking of which, please release her. She's no longer a threat."

"On it, boss," Ship said.

The *D'ru-shaya* link snapped without Moon uttering a word.

Huh.

I could've dwelled on his extended silence, but the theories would get me nowhere. My first priority was kicking Saul into gear.

"How you feel, my friend?"

"Like I was untethered from reality. How long did I sleep?"

"An hour, more or less."

He groaned. "Apologies, Raul. I put our mission at risk."

"On the contrary. That blame falls to me. Senor Vargas is clever. He didn't consider you worthy of skipping the line."

"Excuse me?"

I chuckled. "No worries, my friend. We outwitted him. Horatio never realized the size of his audience. Fortunately, we have a long journey. Enough time for you to recover your faculties and learn what our team in Desperido already knows. Trust me, it's a corker."

Ten minutes out from Todos Santos, I asked Saul what he remembered before he vanished into dreamland.

"Everything. It's very clear until a moment or two after I drank the wine. I was watching you and Horatio banter, then my head went to and fro."

"Had you collected any useful impressions of the man?"

"Oh, yes. I thought he was genuine. I sensed no performance art.

He struck me as sincerely excited to have you in his home."

"Not an impostor, you're saying."

Saul groaned. The man hedged his bets.

"So I assumed. Then he drugged me. Perhaps I've lost my touch at seeing through a mask."

"Not at all. I concluded the same. Still do, oddly enough. The man may yet prove to be a raving lunatic, but I drew the distinct impression he believed everything he said."

Saul, in the dark about what happened down below, replied:

"Does that bode well for us?"

"I'd give it even odds."

We'd know more after the loyalty test.

"Relax, Saul, and enjoy the ride. I'll tell you a very interesting story once we're clear of Todos Santos."

I wasn't thrilled to enter the stone town unarmed, though I knew a tragic outcome was about as likely as being struck down by Ixoca.

The town's population, sparse in the late morning, had all but vanished indoors. The two young shepherds who also enjoyed blast rifles herded their sheep through a narrow lane while we waited. They ignored us.

We passed into an empty town square.

"This must be nap time," I joked.

I drove the chaser to the archway through which the saucer-eyed boy said he lived with his mother. He appeared before I dropped Whisper's ballast.

Still in his white robe, the kid presented me with a woven basket. Inside, I saw two pistols, my pom, and a ball of dark cheese wrapped in a translucent cloth.

"Thank you for trusting me," the boy said. "My father said you were a respectful man. Please accept this cheese. It's our specialty."

"I appreciate the gesture. Your name is?"

He sealed those lips.

"You are the oldest son to Senor Vargas?"

No words, but a slight nod.

"I hope we see each other again someday. Goodbye, my young friend, and thank you."

"Good day, Senor."

He retreated through the archway.

"Whatcha think, Saul? A tad bit off?"

"More than."

I scoped the empty square.

"I do believe we need to learn about this town."

Saul nodded. "What are you thinking, boss?"

"It's important somehow. Important to Vargas, anyway. That might be good enough."

As we exited the town, I felt a disquieting shudder.

Were those goosebumps?

Huh. My syneth never produced that effect before.

*"Theo, was that you just now?"*

He ignored me.

*"Theo, are you playing games with me?"*

Three knocks against my consciousness preceded a sleepy voice.

*"We are trying to console Addis. She will be permanently scarred by this experience."*

*"That's not what I asked."*

*"You told us to leave you in peace, Royal. We did."*

I didn't care for his transition to third person pronouns.

*"I'll take your word, Theo. Return to your business."*

He said nothing the rest of the journey home. Theo was the least of my concerns. Chief among them: Convincing Moon to buy into my glorious new vision of the future.

However, Moon spent those four hours anticipating my proposal and threw it back in my face the moment we had private time.

"The credits are important," Moon said, "but you're focused on the Jewel of Eternity. You want it for yourself."

"For both of us."

Moon didn't strike an insurgent tone. He knew the money would buy a small army and stamp passage to wherever we intended to set up permanent shop.

"I'll do whatever it takes to secure those creds, Royal. Any human that stands between us and our fortune is dead. But this Jewel is a distraction. If we find it, we hand it over to Vargas and his people. We take their money, and we leave Azteca for good."

"Along with our lieutenants and other loyal followers. Yes?"

He nodded while pulling on his cigar.

"We build our syndicate from the ground up. Just like we always envisioned, Royal. It's the only reason we endured nineteen years in the desert."

Everything he said made perfect sense. This job trumped the need to work for the President any longer. Combined with the ten percent I'd been skimming off the top of Desperido's illicit profits, we'd have roughly twenty-seven million UCVs at our discretion.

More if I negotiated a higher payoff with Vargas.

I titillated at the thought.

Yet it wasn't enough by a longshot.

"Moon, all those credits will not change one fundamental truth: We are shells of what we used to be. We were exposed before Desperido and worse off now. But with a Jewel? We can chart a new path to a different type of godhood. I believe *Father and Mother* sent us here to find the Jewel. We will walk among humans without fear of death. The Jewel of Eternity will be our invincibility cloak, my friend."

He wanted to believe me. I heard it in his voice.

"We can't be certain it's real. His evidence was pitiful. That image could have been manipulated."

"Theo confirmed the match. It was a Jewel core matrix."

"Vargas may be using a stolen image from old Chancellor research, or even from the Aeternans."

I had considered the possibility on the trip home.

"Scratch the immortals off your list. They won't even publicly acknowledge the Jewels are responsible for terraforming Aeterna. They only opened their system to scientific research less than ten years ago, but even that's tightly controlled. They'll never grant mortals the access to their biggest secrets."

"Vargas claims his people are wealthy. A big payoff ..."

"No. Those self-righteous immortals don't concern themselves with UCVs. They barter for goods and services. The rest they manufacture themselves. I could offer their Minister fifty million creds for a single hectare of land, and he'd order me to leave."

"What of the Chancellors?"

A slightly trickier case to make, but I tried.

"You heard Vargas. They suppressed research for centuries."

Moon grunted. "Until they found the Jewels themselves."

Ah, yes. The tricky bit.

Moon was right. When we were the Wolf and Serpent gods, we saw the story play out across the continuum. Chancellor explorers captured the Jewels outside Collectorate space about ninety standard years ago and conducted research.

Typical reckless humans. They never realized they were dealing with a sentient form of life. They focused on weapons potential. When that came up dry, the Jewels fell into the hands of the same two assholes who gave life to bioengineered immortals like me: Emil and Frances Bouchet.

Their caste was dying of a genetic collapse, so they tasked themselves with merging Jewel energy to humans. They created ten prototypes for a new breed of Chancellor. As usually happened when humans aspired to godhood, it all went tits-up. Those prototypes caused a world of hurt.

And down went the Chancellory's empire. Shortly after that, down went the prototypes.

Many Jewels avoided capture. They'd been busy in this sector for a million years transforming planets and building a wormhole network called the Fulcrum. That network gave the human race quick access to other systems. The Jewels turned Hiebimini into a lifeless rock seventy years ago, forcing the residents to evacuate. They refashioned it in time for my immortal brethren to claim it as Aeterna thirty-one standard years ago.

I rehashed all this history with Moon, concluding with:

"The Bouchets were executed, and their records destroyed. The Aeternans won't surrender their secrets. So, Vargas has had no access to the Jewel matrix. The image is real, Moon, and it's ancient."

He shot back without missing a beat.

"Suppose it is, partner. Now, let's take it another step. There really is a Jewel living beneath this planet calling itself Ixoca. And Vargas knows where to find it. We take the job and retrieve Ixoca. What then? Hand it over and collect our twenty million. Yes?"

I winked. "That's the plan, my friend."

"Then, after he's paid us, we come back for Ixoca. We steal it and slaughter everyone who gets in our way. Sound good?"

"Perfect."

"We leave with our lieutenants for parts unknown and then ...? What next? You expect us to merge with that Jewel, don't you?"

I confirmed my plan at risk of sounding like a megalomaniac (which, in fairness, I was for much of my godly romp across the heavens).

"Moon, imagine syneth and our consciousness blended with that core matrix. The Creators' knowledge combined with the Jewel's millions of years of experience. We'll have the power to create and destroy on a global scale. Better yet, Vargas claims Ixoca broke off pieces of itself into its followers. Imagine if we could do the same. Tell me you're not excited."

The hunger in his smile burned bright. The last time I saw it so fully formed, Moon watched more than two hundred people go to their fiery deaths on Qasi Ransome.

"A few months ago, I'd have given anything for this," he said. "If it meant becoming a god again? Away from this rock?"

"But now?"

"My dreams haven't changed. I have. You taught patience and discipline. You taught me to slow down and analyze all the angles first. I listened, Royal. Then I watched you violate those principles and damn near get us both killed. Today, you spent an hour with a fanatic who's dreaming of ... damn if I know what Vargas intends. You haven't learned your lesson, partner. Lunatics with tattoos cannot be trusted."

Fair point. I took on a massive chest tattoo when I was a teen and killed for a gaggle of terrorists. Our target: Outsiders. Moon and I fought a Swarm empire where billions of brainwashed adherents wore a scorpion on their right cheek to avoid joining the billions of others that the Holy Risen Church slaughtered. We wore lovely scalp tattoos of the Wolf and the Serpent when we annihilated the last thirty million Creators and two billion humans in the Beta universe.

Humans and gods were equally adept at repeating history.

"My friend, trust doesn't enter into it. The road has been paved. *Father and Mother* placed us on Azteca to meet this moment."

"You don't know that, Royal."

"I do. This timeline is a gift. A thank-you for reinstating reality as *Father and Mother* intended it."

Moon poured himself a drink.

"The only thing we know about *Father and Mother* is that it wanted the universes for itself, and it kicked our asses." He held the glass to his nose and sniffed the whiskey. "You think Ixoca is *what?* A consolation prize?"

No better time for honesty.

"Yes, Moon. We'll never have a better offer. We're heroes, you and I. We saved these goddamn humans, and we never received due credit. For years, you clung to the edge of sanity with your bare fingernails. We dug pralones for water in the middle of the desert. We took crumbs from a President who will die within a year. We deserve proper reparation.

"But this is even better, my friend. It's evolution. There'll be nothing like us in the universes. We won't need to be heroes. We will pick and choose our targets, and no one will stop us."

I spoke Moon's language better than he articulated it. Judging from his softened features, he appreciated how I seasoned my words with a tiny pinch of madman and a dollop of vengeance.

"You thought I'd gone soft, Moon. Yes, I'm fond of Elian, Ship, Saul, and Genoa. I've enjoyed my time in Desperido. But I never lost sight of the plan and why we deserve it. This Jewel is the turnkey. Every gram of syneth tells me so."

He finished his drink and set the glass aside.

"I want to believe you, Royal. That's all I did for the last two thousand years – believe you. Take your damn word at face value. I was the partner who followed."

Push came to shove, he'd do so again.

"Until recently, you never regretted it, Moon. I gave you pause. Now we're back on track. Vargas is the key. Our future starts with him. We'll pass his loyalty test then move on to the adventure of our newest lives."

Did I close the sale? Moon didn't say no, which was a positive. For the time being, we agreed on how much to tell our lieutenants. I hated withholding anything from these folks. That night, we sat inside Bart and allowed them to toss out a stream of random questions until they were duly satisfied. We only lied once or twice.

We studied Horatio's profile, including his business interests and family history. He was a good little general, keeping his nose clean and building a wide swath of contacts in the public and private arenas. Not the first hint of scandal or criminal activity.

We went about our daily routines and waited.

Then waited some more.

I chalked up the delay to Horatio being a careful man. His people knew a thing or two about discipline. If Vash hadn't crossed the line to strike a deal with the Horax, that little asshole would still be alive.

Two road trains came and went, filling hold three with almost a million creds in product. At the current pace, Elian would surpass Moon and I for richest man in Desperido in a few months.

I told Lumen she was free to leave. Her usefulness had dried up. But for inexplicable reasons, she clung to the cantina.

The days were quiet. No Horax, no investigators, no melodrama.

In other words, about as dull as life in the ruins of a desert fort.

Frank Kennedy – Blue Heart

Everything changed on the seventeenth day.

# 12

**Standard Day 1, SY 5390**

GENOA NEVER FOUGHT IN THE WAR, but she enjoyed my tales of battling the Swarm. They were gruesome, and I censored nothing for her benefit. On the contrary, she used my experience as fuel for the combat she hoped to see one day. The defense of Road Train 1492 filled her with purpose.

"Your time will come," I said. "We'll be taking on nasty business in the very near future."

I made that promise as we walked the perimeter. The dog days since meeting with Horatio forced me to find creative outlets to fill the hours. I often walked with our militia while they were on duty.

"Off world?" She asked.

"That's the goal."

"Good. I'm not much of an Aztecan. Always figured I was meant for more."

"And better, my friend. It's a new year, fraught with possibility."

The instant I said it, the first possibility burst onto our long-range trackers. I received a beacon to my pom and followed the motion of a single, four-wheeled flatcar bearing south through the Ogala Hills. Genoa moaned.

"Another investigator?"

"Unlikely. They haven't bothered us for weeks."

I didn't want to raise my hopes unfairly. Horatio never said how his messenger would arrive. Just as likely, the driver made a wrong turn somewhere and was too damn stubborn to admit it. That happened on occasion. Four Desperidans once stumbled into town and chose not to turn around.

This approach differed from the others. The flatcar stopped half a kay shy of the outer shield. Someone stepped out and tapped the roof, which retracted. The vehicle returned north, and the passenger hoofed toward us.

"Thoughts?" I asked Genoa.

"The driver is scared of Desperido. We built a rep, boss."

"In many quarters."

My pom linked to a perimeter drone sighter. It zoomed in on our lone visitor, who I couldn't identify behind thick black goggles, a wide-brimmed hat, and a blue/gray dust jacket that struck me as familiar. The walker, who was short but thick around the waist, toted a full backpack and moved along at an eager pace.

My enthusiasm dwindled. This creature likely wasn't anyone's messenger. I began to believe Horatio's "loyalty test" was seeing how long we would wait around.

"What now, boss? Meet them halfway, find out their business?"

I tapped my ear bead.

"Partner, how's the work coming?"

"Done," Moon said. "I was about to take Ship for a training run."

"Perfect. Join us at the north perimeter. There's someone coming. Let's give them a proper Desperido welcome."

"On it."

Out of Moon's boredom had come a delightful idea: Arm the overland chasers with gun turrets. The vehicle designs weren't compatible with such add-ons, but our syneth core contained the records of every human (and non-human) weapons innovation.

Moon needed a project to keep his mind sharp and his instinct for blood at bay. He installed retractable forward turrets that worked through the digital Nav board.

The chaser Red Dust arrived with our newcomer still a couple hundred meters from the perimeter. He and Ship hopped out.

"Who's this?" Moon asked.

"Someone with nowhere else to go, I suspect."

"Sure ain't the first, boss," Ship added. "I seen others enter town the same way. All alone on Roadway 9. One fella – Jem – walked straight from Machado about three years ago."

I searched my memory.

"Jem? Name isn't familiar."

"Oh, he didn't last six weeks. Poor asshole was fed a pile of bull about Desperido. Told we were a paradise off the grid. When Jem realized he'd have to work to make do, he packed up his shit and scrammed sometime middle of the night."

These days, "paradise off the grid" hued a little closer to reality. Our contractors were making big money; even those not affiliated with Motif saw residual benefits. Their wares drew higher prices on the night market when packaged with Motif canisters. I fully expected a wave of unsavory types on a pilgrimage to join our little operation. That wave had yet to materialize. Was this walker the first of many?

"Ship, why don't you take Nav on Red Dust. Open the turrets when this poor soul is within twenty meters."

His enthusiasm turned to quick confusion.

"Sure, boss. Uh. You actually want me to gun 'em down?"

"No, no. We'll make them understand the price of admission."

He smiled with evident relief.

"Gotcha, boss. Good policy."

Ship disappointed me. Where was the killer instinct?

The walker straddled the center of the road and did not slow for a greeting party of three armed Aztecans and a hovering craft with guns in full view. Something jingled on the visitor's belt.

Inside twenty meters, I recognized the blue/gray jacket.

"UNF flight jacket," I told Moon.

"Active duty?"

"Too weathered."

The walker reached inside the jacket and retrieved a palm-sized object, out of which flipped a sweet little knife. He or she pointed the blade at each of us but did not slow.

I assumed our silence would send a clear message.

Yeah, no.

"Lay a hand on me," a woman said, "and you'll see."

Her voice was deep, hewn out of a rough goddamn rock. I heard it before. The rest of the woman's getup suddenly made sense.

Was she fearless or bluffing?

I chose both.

"What's your business in Desperido?" I paused then added: "Bett."

The woman focused her blade on me as she removed her goggles. Her hat shaded her features from the sun, but her war injuries stood out. A scar snaked across her left forehead. The lens in her prosthetic left eye didn't match her right.

"Motherfucking Raul. Wasn't sure I'd find you here."

"Good to see you on your feet, my friend."

She stopped just shy of the all-bets-are-off zone.

"Don't even try that silky smooth shit on me. Last time, I took a bolt to the chest."

"A regrettable misfortune." To my team, I said: "This is MaryBeth Ortiz, although she prefers Bett. You'll recall she was the northbound Nav for Road Train 1492."

Bett shot Moon a dangerous side-eye. The last time she saw him, Moon carried her to the break room for placement in a phasic trauma pod. He saved the woman's life, but gratitude was not on her agenda.

"All you malgados were on my train. What say I take you lot out in the desert one at a time and give thanks?"

I narrowed my choice: This woman was fearless.

Then again, she had nothing to lose.

"Bett, I hope you haven't come to our fair town looking for revenge. It will end badly. For you, I fear."

She closed the knife and dropped it in a pocket.

"I thought about rounding up my old unit. We'd jump into town at night, go from house to house."

"But you knew that was impractical. I'm certain you did your homework. You heard what happened to the Horax."

She wanted to spit on me. I heard the suction as Bett gathered a nice wad of saliva. Instead, she swallowed her rage.

"Yeah, Raul. I heard." Her eyes shifted to Red Dust. "What in ten hells? Turrets on a chaser? You planning for war?"

"It's an effective design," Moon said, more than a little miffed.

"If you say so." Her grin sprouted disdain.

"Bett, remember my partner Ilan? He carried you to safety."

"Oh, I remember many things, Raul."

"Yes. And according to my sources, you did not hold back in your testimony to Montez and the guild. They had a hard time believing certain details. Bett, I am truly sorry you lost your job."

Bett reached in the same pocket, perhaps contemplating a more decisive blow. Fortunately, she wasn't suicidal.

"Sixteen years I lost because of you fucks."

"And now, you come to us why?"

She laughed. "You owe me. I'll kindly take a share of what you stow in hold three."

"Ah." I shrugged. "Compensation. You might have led with that rather than denigrating our characters."

"I earned the right to denigrate you people."

Fair point. We did have a tendency to ruin lives. At least Bett still had hers.

"Bett, the woman to my right is Genoa. She's outstanding with a rifle and took out many targets that might otherwise have caused great problems for the tumbler."

Genoa held her ground but managed a respectful nod. Bett showed no interest.

"The young man in our chaser is Ship. He too aided in your defense."

She ignored the kid's timid wave.

"Don't make it sound so goddamn honorable. I have friends. They know the real story, Raul. Those pirates hit us because you lot poked the Horax bear."

"True. We did have an unfortunate disagreement. But that matter's been settled. The trains are running without disruption."

"Maybe so, but I ain't one of their Navs. And that's on you."

Our little pissing match could've lasted for hours. It was great entertainment. But MaryBeth Ortiz, with a loaded backpack, did not come this far to rant in the middle of the road.

"Bett, I recall a moment in the cab when we are at odds over deploying the snow smasher. You might remember I introduced myself, said I loved whiskey, and vowed to share a drink with you after our adventure ended. I'd love to follow through."

She studied me with cold (and justifiable) suspicion.

"I could use a drink."

"Perfect. Genoa, why don't you continue with your duties? Ilan and I will escort Bett to the cantina."

"Yes, boss. I ..."

Bett interrupted.

"The fuck you will." She made for the chaser, swung around to the passenger side, and threw her backpack into a rear bucket. "What's your name again, kid?"

Ship glanced between me and Bett.

"Uh, Ship Foster."

She hopped into the front bucket beside him.

"Drive."

I nodded my approval.

"See you there, Bett."

She acknowledged me with her middle finger.

"Well, that's a fine development," I said afterward.

"Why is she really here?" Moon asked.

"You heard her. Compensation."

"She's lying."

"Eh. We all lie. But this woman is out of work, pissed, and laser-focused, my friend. More important, she's whip smart. See, if Montez cited her for incompetence, as Horatio claimed, she'll never get another job in the industry. She's screwed. But she also knows we're rolling in UCVs from our stock."

Ilan grunted. "She wants a payoff."

"No, Ilan. She wants what she deserves. The only question to answer is …"

"How much?"

I chuckled. "And for how long? That's a large backpack. I suspect her entire life resides within. What do you say we join her for a drink and delve a little further?"

He stared at me like I was overlooking the obvious.

"Yes," I said. "It's possible she's a plant."

"We haven't heard from Vargas in seventeen days."

"True. It's also possible those 'friends' she mentioned might have encouraged her to visit Desperido."

"Horax? Montez? Constabulary?"

"Why not select all of the above, my friend? Each as likely as the other. To which I mean, not likely at all."

Her timing interested me from another angle: The next road train arrived in two days. An undercover scout, perhaps?

Eh. No point in allowing my paranoia to roam free.

Typically, I killed anyone who tried to collect a debt. Would today set an historic precedent?

I looked forward to hearing Bett's story.

# 13

**B**ETT FOUND AN EMPTY BOOTH and made herself at home. When we entered the cantina, she lit a white-wrapped cheroot and shouted her preference to the barkeep. Lumen didn't take kindly to such behavior on a good day. Ship held counsel with Lumen, who glanced our direction. By the time Ilan and I slipped into the opposite booth, Ship brought a full bottle of my favorite whiskey plus four glasses.

"Staying, my friend?" I asked the kid.
"If it's good with you, boss."
"Think your belly can handle it?"
He shaded his eyes from our guest.
"I'm good."
Bett smirked as she pulled on the cheroot. It gave off the sickly sweet smell of piss-poor tobacco. She needed a quality cigar. As for Ship: The kid claimed he drank every day with the intent to build up an iron resistance.
He dragged over a chair when I gave permission to stick around.
I poured the drinks and waited for Bett's critique.
"It'll do," she said, motioning for another.
After we drank, I asked the most pressing question:
"How long do you plan to stay, Bett?"
"Me?" She puffed her lips with indignation. "My ass is firmly

planted, Raul. I ain't leaving – unless you kill me."

"Ah. Long term, is it?"

She removed her hat to reveal the tight cut she wore as a Nav.

"I didn't come this far for a handout. I knew damned well I wouldn't get one even if I threatened to bring holy hell on this town. And, just so we understand: I still can."

A threat or a bluff? I voted for the latter.

"If it's not a payoff you seek, then what's your agenda?"

She couldn't take her eyes off Ship, who shifted his away.

"Are we seriously going to do this in front of the boy?"

Ship reared up his shoulders and took appropriate offense.

"Hey, now. Hold on. I'm …"

"He's our lieutenant, Bett. Ship is a trusted friend."

"Thanks, boss."

Bett shifted her ass on the cushion until she was comfy.

"Who am I to question your chain of command, Raul?"

Moon bit off the end of a cigar and lit it, albeit with a standard fireflick. Too soon to display one of his special skills.

"You won't question anything we do here," my partner said. "If you plan to live until sunset, answer our questions."

That seemed slightly provocative, although it didn't change Bett's disposition. She drank while smoke poured through her nostrils.

"Good. Ask away, malgados. I got nothing to hide."

I did so enjoy the lip on this one. She'd never be accused of elegant discourse, but that was my particular talent. I wasn't looking for a linguistic peer.

"Why stay?" Moon asked. "We could fill your account now and send you north."

"That's one solution. Ilan, is it? Yeah. Pay me off and save yourselves time, money, and aggravation. No, senor. What I'm due is a thousand times more lucrative."

"Which is what?" I asked.

She polished off the second glass. I pushed the bottle her way.

"A stake in your operation."

I suspected she might go there.

"What's the appeal? We're a small town at the anus of Azteca. What we're doing right now is the height of entertainment around here."

She chuckled. "You don't play humble well at all. Look, I ran Nav my last trips through here. I never reviewed the hold three manifest, but I saw the size of your cases before they were loaded."

"Ah. And what was your expert assessment?"

"There's gold underneath all that dust. Your top earner pulls more UCVs in a single run than I made in a standard year. I'm tired of playing a game I can't win."

"Interesting. Let's take a step back. Montez fired you weeks ago. I assume you were blackballed."

She grabbed the bottle and poured.

"That was the least painful part."

"Go on."

"Montez paid off my crew for their silence. No one validated my version of events."

"Including Nestor, the other Nav?"

Bett snickered. "That weaselly fucker. They wanted him to play the hero, so he gave them a show. He said I didn't properly secure the holds or my cab from intruders. He said I panicked. And then, after they pressed him about you, that malgado told them some load of shit about a connection between the cartels and the shipping groups. He said your team was investigating a threat to global security."

Which was, essentially, what I told him to say. I wasn't sure he'd have the testicles for it. Or that he'd bury Bett under a stack of fiction.

Oh, yes. Nestor had the stomach of a fine corporate executive. Or worse, a politician.

"My sincerest apologies, Bett. I never ..."

"Fuck you and your apologies, Raul."

"Noted. I assume you protested their decision?"

"For what it was worth."

"Did Montez offer you severance?"

That warranted a chuckle.

"Three lousy goddamn months. They revoked my pension."

Even by corporate standards, the punishment seemed harsh.

"Bett, why didn't they simply remove you from field service? Montez is a massive entity. They could've slotted you in an office."

She tugged at her jacket, which bore the logo of a UNF Hornet fighter squadron.

"Why do you think?"

I was genuinely stumped. Neither Moon nor Ship bailed me out.

"What's the connection between your UNF service and ...?"

"Hah. You don't know. Do you?"

I threw up my hands in surrender.

"I'm at a loss."

"Raul, you said you served in the war. Was that bullshit?"

"Not at all. So did my partner, after a fashion."

"The fuck does that mean?"

An awkward moment. I could've said I fought the Swarm in another universe during another life then effectively destroyed them in this universe.

Yeah, no. Too much information.

Our lack of response triggered a wry grin.

"Who did you serve under?" She asked.

Not even the High Admiral held sway over us. Again, too soon.

"Oh, I get it," she said after another pause. "You two were SI."

We didn't deny the accusation, which satisfied her.

"Figures. A pair of mules nobody's ever heard of, taking on the Horax and who knows what all. Hiding out here off the grid, running the show. The constabulary won't touch you. Montez keeps your resupply tumbler running on schedule. A hell of a setup."

"Yes. Well. One makes do. Back to this business about your service, Bett. Explain the problem."

She dived into her third drink. When she came up for air:

"It's an open secret among vets. They're pushing us out."

"Who is?"

"The major corporations. The continental governments. They've been easing out vets for years."

"Why? You defended Azteca from the Swarm. This planet alone lost seventy thousand in the fight."

"Old news. War ended nineteen years ago. People don't want to hear about those days anymore."

Interesting, but not terribly surprising. Humans had a long tendency to distance themselves from wars until they forgot the old lessons and started new conflicts.

"I don't see why your livelihoods should be endangered by changing attitudes."

"Beats the fuck out of me, Raul. But it's happening all over Azteca. Six good men and women from my Hornet squadron got tossed on their asses in the past two years. They had great jobs, long careers, nice pensions down the road."

"All civilian?" She nodded as she sipped. "Do you collect retirement from the UNF?"

"Only served three years. One tour rotation don't qualify. You ought to know that shit."

"I do. Yes. I'm curious. Have you heard of this happening off world?"

"Don't know."

"Have you considered reapplying to the UNF?"

That drew the loudest chuckle yet.

"Look at me, Raul. I'm a wasted cunt. Besides, the UNF operates at twenty percent of war capacity. There ain't much call for Hornet pilots these days."

"So, you've been kicked to the curb with no serviceable options except what we allegedly offer in Desperido. Yes?"

Bett buried her face in her uprisen hands.

"Yeah, Raul. That's the size of it. I got nothing left out there. No family, no job, and a giant goddamn knife in the back." She bandied her rage-filled eyes between Moon and I (Ship might as well have been on another planet). "I'm so desperate I decided to see if the assholes who ruined my life had something better to offer."

She struck me as utterly credible, and her story about veteran firings just strange enough to intrigue me. Bett came to our town fully energized with the disillusion and rage that brought so many Aztecan misfits to Desperido.

It was perfectly suited for her audience.

Which was, of course, the biggest problem with her story.

"What is it you think we can offer, Bett?"

She poured drink number four and stubbed out her cheroot.

"A fresh damn start, for one. That's the least you owe me."

"Second?"

"Peace and quiet. I reckon you'll have that covered."

"True, to a point. The people in this town don't sit out all night watching the stars then sleep until midday. We have a vibrant economy underground. Everyone works for a living."

Bett threw back her whiskey in one shot and burped.

"Peace and hard work ain't mutually exclusive. And I am not without talent. I'll contribute."

"Third?"

"I like a firm mattress. My back was never the same after the war. Small space, firm mattress."

I turned to Ship.

"No one's moved into your old room, have they?"

"It's free," the kid said. "And the mattress is like a slab of rock."

"Sounds perfect." Bett pushed the bottle toward me. "That'll do me for now. I feel a piss coming on."

"One thing, Bett. The room is in the back of the cantina. And if you want to make an honest contribution, I happen to know our barkeep is in need of assistance."

It wasn't the smartest recommendation I ever made. Those two coits would be warring within the hour.

Bett scoped the place.

"Easy enough. I worked a few red lights before the war."

"Lovely. I'll smooth things over with Lumen when we're done here. There's just one matter we need to resolve, Bett."

She crossed her arms on the table and gave me a cold stare.

"The fuck is that, Raul?"

"If you needed a room and a job, you could've asked when we met on the road. Instead, you've done little but antagonize and demean in a most profane manner. There's an old phrase that goes back centuries. 'If you want to gather honey, don't kick over the beehive.' While your anger is understandable, you put your own life in great jeopardy with an ill-advised strategy."

She did not flinch. Damn, this woman was starting to rub off.

"Ill-advised? That's what you think? All that schmoozing you did in my cab – it weren't an act. You're always like this."

"Compliment noted."

Bett took her eyes off us for a few seconds, looking around to see who else might be listening. Satisfied, she lowered her voice.

"I don't know what you are, Raul. Or you, Ilan. But I aim to find out. You can come clean, or I'll snoop until I know your secret."

"I'm confused. Secret?"

"You took multiple laser bolts at point-blank range. Nobody comes back from that."

"Ah, yes. My contact said you made the claim to your superiors and added how I walked off the train in fine spirits. Truth is, Bett, I wore heavy armor beneath my clothes. Specially designed to repel laser energy. Simple."

"Fuck you. I took a glancing blow and thought I'd die. But I heard every word you said." She pointed to my partner. "You called him forward. You told him you were dying. You were so bad off, your partner here had to chase down Nestor."

"The injuries weren't as dreadful as I imagined. Ilan, he ..."

"Raul's armor absorbed the bolts," Moon said. "He broke a few ribs and struggled to breathe. That's all."

She didn't believe a word.

"I couldn't move on my own, so I didn't see shit behind me. But you had no business walking off my train alive, Raul. Give me a legitimate explanation – something I can believe – or I'll be up your business every goddamn, insufferable day."

I doubted that would represent a change in her normal routine.

"Huh. If you intend to be a nuisance rather than a contributing member of this town, we'll need to discuss your timely exit."

"My ass is planted right here, Raul."

Was that an opening for a witty retort?

"I'll speak with Lumen. If you're committed to this course, she'll provide you with a blanket, a pillow, and a bottle for your piss."

She laughed, but the mockery was evident.

"Give me quarters, and I'll carry my weight. Then we'll discuss options, including how big a stake I'm owed."

I pivoted to Moon.

"Thoughts, partner?"

He spoke to me but stared at Bett.

"This one's your call, partner. You're at the top of her hit list."

"Good point. We'll give you a free trial, Bett. But try not to overstep. The desert is unforgiving."

Bett squirmed. "That where you hide all the bodies?"

I dropped my congenial smile. "Yes. About a hundred so far."

"We prefer cremation," Moon added with no hint of irony.

A few awkward, quiet seconds followed. If she was a spy, Bett went forward fully aware of the price for betraying Desperido.

"Before you settle in, my friend, we'll need to search your belongings. And we'll have to scan you for any misplaced anomalies. No weapons, no comms until we say different."

Bett shrugged me off.

"Your town, your rules."

Perhaps the liquor took hold. Then again, Bett struck me as a woman who could drink most anyone under the table.

Lumen resisted my effort to house Bett in Ship's old quarters and add her to the cantina's paystamps. She dropped her fight when I reminded her of two things: One, Lumen forfeited her leverage when

I met with Horatio Vargas. Two, the town expected their barkeep to possess an unpleasant demeanor. They wouldn't notice the difference if I installed Bett in the role.

"Her tongue is sharp as a razor," I added. "Don't underestimate the entertainment value."

Shortly afterward, I settled inside Bart to develop a profile on our newest resident. Moon joined me.

"She's clean," he said.

"Interesting. No link to the outside world?"

"Nothing. Just personals."

"Exactly what you might expect from someone intent on a fresh start. A perfect candidate for Desperido. Do you buy it?"

"I don't trust any human."

I chuckled. "Sad, isn't it? The only ones who don't plot against us are tools. Bett intrigues me, Moon. She was a professional soldier. She knows combat – the kind where survival is a second-by-second ordeal. Plus, if she considers herself betrayed by a world she fought to protect, then any option is fair game. That business about the veterans is odd. We can exploit it and bring her along."

"What are you saying? The table?"

"In time. She already believes we're SI protected by powerful forces. If she knew the full extent of our ability, Bett just might decide to suit up for a new team."

"You're getting ahead of yourself, Royal. Again. We can't dismiss the timing. Quiet for seventeen days, and then this apparent gift walks into town on her own?"

Moon always made sense, which is why I had to fight him.

"That's causality for you, my friend. A beautiful knot."

"You still believe *Father and Mother* saw it coming?"

I glanced at the first data spools retrieved on MaryBeth Ortiz.

"The pieces are aligning. Bett is on the board now. We'll hear from Vargas any day. Preparation, patience, and poise will prevail."

Or so I told myself.

Events two days later suggested otherwise.

# 14

ELIAN CAME TO ME AT SUNRISE, a few hours before the resupply tumbler was due. Poor fella hadn't slept all night. The previous day, he'd been off his game during inventory of product lines. He was unnaturally quiet given the size of this week's shipment, his best yet.

He joined me at my usual spot on the eastern perimeter. I had begun a new routine after my trip to Vargas Vineyards. With a whiskey-spiked café in hand, I made a daily promise to the sun.

"Take a good look. I won't be here much longer."

Elian arrived seconds after I repeated that vow.

"I'm exhausted, boss."

"You do look ragged, my friend." He blew his nose. "Coming down with something?"

"It's anxiety. I have these attacks. I start sneezing, and I can't stop. Zaps the hell out of me, boss."

His lack of color suggested he ought to be lying down.

"You do look frightful. Tell me, Elian. What's the cause?"

"Success."

I chuckled and finished my café.

"Ah. Demand is exceeding supply. Yes?"

"Ain't even close, boss."

"You're learning a valuable lesson: Winning is a temporary salve. With victory comes high expectations, and expectations become harder to meet."

He sounded out of breath.

"We're maxed out, boss. We can't expand production without new space and equipment. Everybody on my team is working until they drop, but quality control is suffering."

Good thing misfits and ne'er-do-wells weren't banging at our doors. Desperido ran out of vacancies after our most recent arrival.

"I heard you commandeered the last empty cubes."

"We did, boss. Some of my people have doubled up, but it's not enough. We need to build on the surface or ..."

He tailed off.

"Or?"

"Raul, you said we'd expand off world eventually."

Right on cue. He'd been skirting around the subject for days.

"We're much closer, Elian. After we complete the mission for Vargas, we'll consider new locations for your operation. Ilan and I discussed a few potential sites."

"You have?"

"Nothing concrete. What's the phrase for it? *Spitballing.* Yes. We've been spitballing locations."

"Good to hear. Any planets in particular?"

As much as I trusted Elian – and everyone at our table – certain information remained at need-to-know status. They might balk if they knew the meat of those discussions.

For another time ...

"Elian, how much Motif has shipped off world?"

"Best guess? Less than five percent. We got a strong domestic setup on Azteca. The road trains, the night market, and the cartels work together real well. But the interstellar game is a mess. UNF regulations, customs checks, unreliable smugglers. Everybody works their own angle. If our clients don't find the right off-world contacts ..."

I slapped him on the shoulder.

"The trouble can find its way back here. Understood. We need to build our own network of independent contractors."

"That's the size of it, boss. A single cartel with an active footprint on every Collectorate world."

"In the meantime," I said, preferring not to share what I knew about the future, "consider slowing production."

Elian gasped. "Sure about that, boss?"

"You've exceeded projections for the first six weeks. Hold the line and raise the prices. Simple economics."

"How will our buyers react?"

"By passing along the costs to their customers. Humans are weak, my friend. They'll pay any price for a thrill."

"Even when they know the risk."

"Especially then. Have you monitored death reports?"

After the initial shipments, I assigned Elian to study the global stream for trends pertaining to drug overdoses and mysterious heart failures. Motif killed a small percentage of users. As long as the number fell in line with other drugs of choice, its presence wouldn't be proclaimed a health crisis. We couldn't afford new scrutiny until we established an interstellar network.

"I think we're good, boss. It's less than four percent. That's below half the original projection."

"Excellent. Why don't you catch a few winks before the tumbler arrives? I want you fresh for the transaction."

"Sure, boss." He swung about and came right back. "Oh, there's one other matter. I've been talking to the new woman. Bett."

Or she talked to him. Bett enjoyed her role as a conduit between the town and its liquor. She chatted up patrons like a human sieve.

"How do you find her, Elian?"

"Speaks her mind. She's a waste in Ship's old job. Bett was in the guild for sixteen years. Before that, a soldier. Did you know the UNF stationed her in five different star systems? Raul, she has contacts."

"Told you about them, did she?"

"Not as such. But it stands to reason."

I was fond of Elian. He meant well.

"She's also been in town two days, my friend. It's a bit soon to allow her inside our more sensitive operations. Yes?"

Elian dropped his shoulders.

"Oh, yeah. Shit. Sorry, boss. I got ahead of myself."

"Your instinct isn't wrong, Elian. Bett may yet be of great use. But we need to see where her loyalties lie. Now, to bed with you."

So much for my time alone with the rising sun. I found Moon inside Bart, where he'd worked for several hours, and proclaimed:

"I intend to issue an edict to the table. No one disturbs Raul when he's drinking café and talking to the fire god of the heavens."

Moon scoffed. "That will inspire confidence."

I chuckled, but Moon couldn't muster a grin at his own sarcasm.

"It seems Bett has been quite the chatty sort, my friend. What's the status on her UNF files?"

"Bart and Addis pulled them an hour ago. Finally."

We developed a profile after Bett arrived, but penetrating UNF service records proved more challenging than the usual governmental or corporate data spools. Moon ordered Addis to break off a piece of herself and aid in the search. Contrary to Theo's protestations that Addis "suffered in agony," Moon said she acclimated to the process and quite enjoyed it. She claimed it was like "getting out of the house for a change." I didn't care so long as we scraped the intel.

"Anything of interest?"

"Not much beyond what she told us. She signed on at first chance, a good two years before the war. Trained in Hornet combat. Ran ninety-five sorties. Lost her eye in the final battle over Hokkaido. She was honorably discharged a year later."

"Huh. Hokkaido, you say? Interesting. I showed up there briefly, as you'll recall. Who was her Captain?"

"Adm. Len Sing."

My so-called heart sank. I had hoped to hear the name of an old friend who I visited that day with a special message. Had Bett been stationed on his warship, she would've been among the audience at our grand performance that both ended the war and shifted reality.

Would've made converting her to our cause a little simpler.

"Name doesn't ring a bell. How did her commanders rate her? Any special commendations?"

He lifted a holo with an entire screen of recognitions.

"According to this, Royal, she was one of the best."

"The discharge. Was it for her injury?"

"When UNF began the first wave of downsizing forces, most Hornet fighters were reassigned. She was offered a job in the Aztecan central recruiting office but resigned her commission. Told her commanding officer she didn't fit well behind a desk."

Damn, I liked this woman. If only I could trust her.

"That tracks. She ran Nav on tumblers for sixteen years at Montez. She loves freedom and has a penchant for surviving close calls with the abyss. Just the skillset we'll need down the way."

Moon swiped away the holo.

"The same skillset makes her a perfect spy."

"True. But we did find evidence to support her claim about veteran discrimination. Their voices are growing louder. Possibly, it's a misdirect, but an intriguing trend. Let's keep a close eye. She's bound to show her colors."

Our wait did not last long.

The resupply tumbler arrived four hours later. Our largest load to date awaited hold three. Per policy after Road Train 1492, only our militia attended the transactions — and they wore sidearms. The tumbler crew in coveralls and dark glasses also wore pistols. It was a form of mutually assured death should anyone act with reckless abandon. We reached this informal agreement with Montez investigators in order to keep the trains on schedule.

Trust, one might say, was in limited supply.

However, profits overrode such petty concerns.

I shared time with Elian reviewing the auditor's manifest. His product alone accounted for eighty percent of our revenue. He deserved the chance to review the payout before I signed off. All went well. Several rifters worth of cases added to everyone's bottom line. I had no qualms with the independent agents – some funded through the Children of Orpheus. The guild crew, however, were unpredictable. Though none from 1492 were allowed to work this route, all had no doubt heard the stories. They shared no love for our quaint little town.

When the last case loaded, I sent Elian away to celebrate with his team. However, the hold three egress did not close on schedule. Another indie crewman jumped off, replacing the auditor. He approached me carrying a wooden box in the palm of his hands.

I tried not to raise my hopes.

"You will not find this item on the manifest," he told me. "It's a personal treasure from one friend to another."

He flipped over the box to display an insignia.

HV.

"What a lovely gift." I accepted the box. "Please tell my friend I will treasure it always."

He nodded and soon disappeared inside hold three. I caught Moon, Saul, Genoa, and Ship with a side-eye. They didn't betray the moment but understood what likely lay inside.

I resisted the sense of urgency to open it. Hold one contained our legitimate supplies, after all. I handed it to Moon and awaited the boring conclusion to our transactions.

Our supplies reflected the town's growing wealth. Aside from a greater volume of kiosk protein pellets, flash-frozen meats and fresh fruit arrived at double our previous order. The cantina's liquor invoice tripled from the week Moon and I took control. An assortment of small luxury items joined the necessities. Our contractors had begun to indulge in the finer things.

As the guild crew offloaded from both holds one and two, I reviewed the manifest. Our bill was eye-popping. Not a problem to pay given our staggering profits on the night market, but something felt off.

The auditor was a squat man who looked silly in the formal white garb, which stretched in unsightly places. I hadn't encountered him before, and he didn't say a word in handing over the tablet.

Yeah, no. Time for a conversation.

"I'd like to inquire about several of these line items. Particularly under the cantina inventory."

Even behind his black glasses, I saw a condescending glare. This asshole expected me to transfer the UCVs pro forma.

Not this time.

"Problem?" He said it with an implicit, "There's no problem."

"Here, for instance."

I zoomed in on four brands of whiskey, including my favorite.

"The price for Barona had been flat at 7.3 creds per liter. Now I see it's 8.8. That is a seventeen percent increase, my friend."

"We don't set the prices, senor."

"So I've been told. But it's interesting. Naruda, Farnel, and H40 have gone up by the same margin. Yet they're distilled by different enterprises. I'm surprised they'd all go up at the same time, by the same amount. It's almost as if they colluded."

In lieu of words, this fella made clicking sounds with his tongue against the roof of his mouth. Did he plan to outwait me? Play that whole I'm-just-the-accountant game? I continued:

"What do you know about potential collusion, my friend?"

The clicking stopped, but his left hand slipped a nudge closer to that holstered pistol.

"Look, senor. I got a job to do and a schedule to meet. Take your complaints where somebody cares."

There were few things more annoying than an accountant who thought himself a tough guy. Give a human a pistol, and suddenly he's Fast-Gun Jose. Did he really like his odds?

"Nice."

I wasn't about to send back the inventory, which was being loaded on rifters. But I also wasn't about to let this wide-bodied creature outwit me. I reviewed the administrative stamp on the manifest and gave this human stump one last chance.

"Ah. Ernesto Carbone. Perhaps we should recast the issue. Who specifically might I consult regarding the unexpected price alterations compared with numbers we received three days ago?"

He appeared to mull a response, but it came out flat and predictable.

"The manufacturers set prices, senor. Prices vary based on quantity and delivery range. Contact the manufacturers."

Moon heard our exchange and edged closer.

"Problem, partner?"

I waved him back with a finger. What irritated me most in the moment? Senor Carbone was half a foot shorter.

Eh. The little guys always carried the biggest chip.

"No problem," I told Moon. "A financial misunderstanding."

Another voice entered the fray from behind.

"The fuck it is!"

Bett had crept onto the scene while we focused on the transactions. This, despite me stopping by the cantina earlier to say she was not allowed to observe when the tumbler arrived.

So much for fitting in and following the rules.

"Bett, if you'd please return to ..."

She ignored me. Of course.

"C'mon, Ernie. I know that's you. How in ten hells you still walk upright is beyond me."

The proceedings grinded to a sudden and awkward halt. Hands surged toward pistols like magnets.

"Apologies, Senor Carbone." I pivoted to our disgruntled new assistant barkeep. "Bett, we're trying to complete business. You have no place here."

"The fuck I don't, Raul. I drove these beasts for sixteen years. Learned a few things. And this malgado!" She pushed in between me and the auditor. "C'mon, Ernie. Admit it. You're still working the game. Can't help yourself!"

Carbone removed his glasses and sneered.

"Out of my space, Ortiz."

Lovely. A personal beef. This was certain to end well.

"Bett, would you plea ..."

"He's been running this con for years. Never the same route twice. Hey, Ernie?"

The auditor snatched the tablet away. Not his smartest move.

"Senor, send this lunatic away at once, or I will order my crew to withhold the entire load."

His tone suggested outrage seasoned with a dash of panic.

"You don't have that power, and I haven't rejected the supplies."

"Then apply your pay stamp, senor."

Bett commanded center stage. Seemed only fair to give her thirty seconds to explain her boorishness.

"You have an accusation to make?"

"Your prices suddenly jumped across the board. Am I right?" After I nodded, she continued. "You're looking at a false overlay of the manifest. It's an evasive data scoop program."

"Senor, this woman is a vengeful bitch with a long history of mental depravity. Montez fired her with cause."

Bett tossed that arrow right back in the form of a belly laugh.

"Raul, the second you enter your pay stamp, they pull the UCVs from your account. Except the difference between the true cost and what you pay diverts to a private account through a data offramp. Guys like Ernie been using this trick all over the world. Sometimes, they pocket the difference. Sometimes, they share with their crew. He shared with me. *Once.*"

His cheeks reddened. "I committed no fraud, but Ortiz reported me anyway. I was cleared of her outrageous charge."

"Because it's an unbeatable program, Raul. The elevated invoice disappears from Montez records. All admin sees is the proper invoice and your legal pay stamp."

"Interesting." I reached for the tablet, which the auditor braced against his chest. "Mind if I reexamine the manifest?"

"To stamp it final. Yes."

He let go as if handing over an infant into my care.

If I were alone with my team, I'd order Theo into the device. He'd uncover the scheme in seconds. Without that option, I relied on good old fashioned instinct.

"Senor Carbone, if I contacted the Montez distribution center listed below, would they confirm the uniform rise in prices?"

"Happily."

"Oh. Lovely." I turned to Moon. "You have your pom?"

"I do."

"Contact the Montez regional authority in Machado. Tell them we have an accounting query with Road Train 1750." I read off the tablet. "Auditor Number 28EC-4999-03."

"On it."

The instant Moon opened his pom and pulled up the public comm, our auditor reached for the tablet. This time, I did not relinquish it.

"I would ask you to stop, senor." Predictably, his tone settled to an agreeable pitch. "I'm sure if I reviewed the manifest again, I'd find an error in the payment algorithm. Shouldn't take but a moment."

"No." I held my tongue for the good of all. "I'm sure it won't take long at all. Thank you for investigating."

While Carbone shuffled his fingers across the screen, I watched Bett's rage turn to chest-pumping satisfaction. Thirty seconds later, Carbone returned the tablet with reasonable prices for every item.

"Delightful." Before I selected the pay stamp, I asked Bett: "What else I should be wary of?"

"If you got an hour to spare ..."

"Ah. I see. Senor Carbone, I'm disappointed. Might I suggest that rather than stuffing your pockets with embezzled funds, you might ask your bosses for a pay increase." I tapped the pay stamp and handed over the tablet. "And in the future, I recommend you avoid this route."

He said nothing to me, but I think he might have taken a shot at Bett were he not surrounded by opposing weapons. The guild crew finished their work, and our militia took charge of the rifters. There'd be a hell of a line at the supply depot in an hour.

"If you're looking for thanks," I told Bett, "don't look too hard. Yes, you did the town a favor, but you violated a clear command. As you've learned, we have a hierarchy. Procedures must be followed." She didn't deserve a verbal shellacking, however. "Still, your timing was superb. If Carbone has been doing this for years, how does he get away with it?"

"He picks targets like Desperido. Backwater villages and towns. The ones who can't afford to wait for the next resupply. A few spot the discrepancy. Carbone feeds them the same bullshit. They don't have the luxury to wait for mediation, so they pay extra."

"Huh. People go along with being gouged?"

"They don't take on Montez. Costs time and money they don't got."

"I assume you reported him?"

She planted hands on her hips in a pose that screamed, "Of course, dumbass."

"The guild has rules about financial malfeasance, but their global rep comes first. So, that pirate still works in the field."

"We appreciate the assist, Bett. I'll stop by for a drink later, and you can expand on your list of things I should worry about."

"The bottle's on me, Raul."

I ordered her to the cantina, where Lumen watched the affair unfold from the only door. Road Train 1750 departed as our volunteers hopped on rifters. I huddled with Moon.

"Thoughts, my friend?"

He forced a cynical frown.

"They put on a show."

"The timing was remarkable, yes, but the animosity between them was real. Bett just saved the town four thousand credits."

"I'll give her a pass today." He handed me the box from Horatio Vargas. "I'm more interested in what's inside."

"Our future, my friend. Pass the word to our table: Meet in Bart. Twenty minutes."

Moon lit a fresh cigar.

"On it."

## 15

**S**AUL AND SHIP BOARDED my beautiful sedan thirty minutes later, the last of our table. Ship apologized; setup at the supply depot proved more complicated than usual.

"No worries," I told him. "The town expects their depot to open on time. I assume the queue is already winding."

I glanced through the open egress toward the cantina. Bett stood outside, staring in our direction. Curious or treacherous?

Hmm.

I closed the egress and joined my table for the big moment. The box hadn't left my hand, but I resisted the temptation to open it. Everyone needed to be present.

"Only took him nineteen days," I quipped to a few chuckles. "Let's see what our friend has delivered."

Two objects nestled in soft padding. The first I recognized at once: A data slip shaped into a triangular crystal, capable of interfacing with a pom. The second befuddled everyone: A polished hexagonal stone the length of my thumb. It felt like a marble chip.

"Odd. We'll find out soon enough, I suspect."

Moon and I sat at opposite ends, flanked by our lieutenants. I thought a word of caution was appropriate.

"Do understand: It's possible this man is leading us down the garden path to a dreadful end. Anyone who offers twenty million credits has my attention but not necessarily my trust. Simply put, it's appropriate to be skeptical."

I wanted my team to play devil's advocate at every turn. Gave them the greatest chance for survival.

When I laid the data slip over my pom's projector module, up popped Horatio Vargas, walking between rows of grapevines.

"Raul. Ilan. Thank you for your patience. I'm sure these nineteen days have been long and frustrating. You passed our mutual friend's critical first test. Raul, I told you where to find him, but you didn't explore Ixtapa on your own. He's chosen to reward your discipline."

Interesting. So, Horatio wasn't in control, after all.

"I can't stop you from sharing with other members of your team. And you're welcome to offer them a role in your mission. But I must impress a crucial point: Only the two of you may see this through to the end. Our friend is not interested in the others. Violate his terms, and they won't survive."

Horatio stopped to observe the blue grapes. He picked one, sucked the juice out of it, and tossed away the hull.

"This mission will test more than your loyalty. Our friend wishes to gauge your faith as well. If you succeed, you will see his heart. That's more than anyone beyond our group has ever experienced. The honor should humble you.

"What happens at the end of your journey is between you and our mutual friend. He beckons; not me. I'm his conduit."

*Mutual friend.* Interesting how he never mentioned Ixoca by name. A strategic choice, or a direct order from the Jewel itself?

"I won't lie: The journey will be dangerous. You will return to Todos Santos. Warning! The town is heavily defended – much more than you might have realized on your last visit. Their faith is unbroken. They will martyr themselves to defend our friend's heart from unbelievers. If you enter through conventional means, you won't escape with your lives."

*Todos Santos.* That damn well explained many things, from the boys who weren't quite right to the fresh crop of goosebumps I endured on the way out of town. Ixoca resided there.

"When my message ends, a stack drop with a map and logistics will enter your pom's underlay. All contents on the data slip will be erased. Dispose of it. Study the drop carefully. It's programmed to decay one hour after first viewing.

"Beyond that, I'm not allowed to help. He says my work is done for now. Oh, and I should note: The town will not be warned of your approach. He's testing their resolve as well.

"Raul. Ilan. I hope we'll meet again soon as genuine allies in the greatest cause of our age. Goodbye."

Huh.

Nothing flashy. No sales job. Straightforward about the danger. I almost believed he was totally on the level. If not for my overlong experience with humans, I'd have bought it hook, line, and …

"Thoughts, my friend?" I asked Moon.

He leaned back and contemplated. A far cry from the usual snap judgment, but I liked a reflective partner.

"I want to see the stack drop to know what we're up against."

"Do you trust the man?"

Moon shrugged. "If it's a con, he's a better actor than you." That drew smiles around the table. "One thing bothers me. His son lives there. You met the kid twice. Why wouldn't Vargas warn the town? If his kid comes between us and the Jewel, we'll have to put him down."

Our lieutenants turned rigid at the notion of killing a kid. Even Elian shifted in his seat, which was odd since he watched Moon take out five boys in Machado. Perhaps he deemed it OK if the fallen gods handled the dirtiest business.

"A fair point, my friend. If I square his message with how he described the Jewel's ability to break off pieces of itself into humans, then Horatio is likely following orders. He might be like a general among the Children of Orpheus, but even generals report to someone." To my lieutenants, I added: "Your perspective?"

Genoa jumped in first.

"I'm with Ilan. We need to examine the stack. I'll be straight, Raul. I'll go wherever you tell me, but this shit is playing with my mind. I only got used to working for gods a few weeks ago, now there's this Jewel of Eternity. And that business about seeing its heart. What does that even mean?"

"Good question. Saul?"

Our resident forger sighed.

"Vargas strikes me as a man who's trapped. Ilan's question about not warning the town is valid. I sensed a genuine fear. He's worried about those people – certainly his child – but he believes they serve an important purpose. He called them martyrs. That tells me he's accepted his son's role in whatever lies ahead. The plan doesn't belong to Vargas. Not to any of them. They turned over their fate to Ixoca, for better or worse."

A fine assessment. Exactly why I took him to Vargas Vineyards.

"Nice, my friend. They're undoubtedly a cult, but the charismatic leader with the magic touch is not human. Ship? Elian?"

The kid beat his older friend to the punch.

"Whatever we gotta do, boss, I want to be in the field this time."

"Of course. I did promise after Machado. Elian?"

He should've been on top of the world after recording his best profits today. Yet I saw hesitation.

"Like you said earlier, boss. We got twenty million reasons to follow this guy's instructions. He don't concern me. I wish I could say this felt like nothing but glitter. Maybe it's my paranoid streak acting up, but I don't trust Ixoca. I mean, you told us all about the Jewels and their history. But have they done this before? Digging inside people and passing themselves down for generations? What's the endgame? That's my concern, boss."

He hadn't voiced these valid questions in our nineteen-day limbo.

"You're not paranoid, my friend. The better word is *circumspect*. If it helps, I do believe there's precedent. I knew an Aeternan who once had access to a Jewel. He told me a story about the rise of humanity three thousand years ago. He said a Jewel penetrated an Earther who was later credited with building the Chancellor caste from scratch. According to the story, the Jewel gave this man unnatural intellectual abilities and remained in the blood of his descendants all the way to the fall of Hiebimini seventy years ago.

"According to the Aeternan, it was part of a master plan. Lift the human race, send them to the stars with Chancellors leading the way, colonize the Collectorate, and meet their downfall at Hiebimini. Why they chose to upend the hierarchy, I can't say. The Jewels had millions of years to set an agenda. Godlike. Yes?"

I took care with that story. I personally witnessed the Jewel merge with an early human named Johannes Ericsson during my journey across the continuum and saw the spectacular event that deadened Hiebimini.

My lieutenants didn't need to know that truth. More important, I concealed the Aeternan's name. He'd gone down in recent history for staggering villainy and an act of remarkable sacrifice. If they recognized his name, they might deduce our true identity.

Too soon.

"So," Elian replied, "could that mean the Jewel is plotting something similar for Azteca?"

"We won't know its intent until we meet it. But the Children of Orpheus seem to believe Ixoca is leading them toward great heights. I think it best we examine the stack."

If Ixoca did intend chaos, he found the right pair of partners.

I retrieved the stack and threw open its holo. It displayed survey images of Todos Santos, highlighted the stone walls which allowed for only one direct way inside, then moved outward to the surrounding hills. Graphics demonstrated a suggested landing area two kilometers from the town. Data said the local sighter drones did not extend that far outward. We could enter the area via wormhole without detection.

A definite time-saver.

Much to our surprise, Horatio charted a course through the forest beneath its heavy canopy. We'd cross a narrow stream and zero in on a large sewer drain which emerged from a hillside forty meters beneath the eastern wall. Further graphics highlighted a straight route beneath the city until three drains intersected at a T.

A flashing red beacon said only Ilan and I were allowed to pass that point, continuing west. It also warned of patrols.

End of instructions.

Lovely.

Aside from a few gasps and the obvious "Is that it?", practical questions rose immediately.

"What patrols?" "How often?" "How many?"

Those discussions led to more questions.

"What happens after you two leave us?" "How long do we have to hold them off?" "Isn't that T a death trap?"

I studied the marble chip. Horatio never explained its purpose. Did he assume we'd know? Or was this one of life's goddamn frustrating moments when instructions lacked the single item necessary for success?

So many answers. So many unknowns.

We debated scenarios, chief among them the size of the team Moon and I would bring along. Small and nimble would draw the least attention. In that scenario, the universe would likely laugh at us and deliver crushing resistance. However, overwhelming force – bringing along perhaps half our militia – would secure the site long enough to hold off their defenses.

Either way, we'd lose people with no guarantee of our own return. Horatio said Ixoca was interested only in my partner and me. It must've known we weren't human. Perhaps even recognized exactly what we once were.

Did that play to our benefit or detriment?

"This might call for the most furtive approach," I announced. "If only Ilan and I enter, we'll have the best chance to skirt around their patrols without detection."

Elian was aghast. "What? No, boss. Not a chance. Vargas left us out to dry. No intel on frequency of patrols or defensive systems."

"I agree," Genoa added. "Simple motion detectors could size you up before you enter the first drain. Once you're inside, they'll come after you from both ends. No way out."

"If we're there," Ship continued, "we'll take them down and give you a chance to finish the mission."

"Your points are valid, my friends. But these drains are not defensible positions, regardless of our numbers. If Ixoca's believers will die for him, then they will be relentless. Some of you will fall. Perhaps everyone. I can't have that – not after what we've built here."

Those were just words, of course. I had no problem with a high casualty rate if we accomplished the mission. Yet selflessness rang sweeter in a human's ear.

Saul offered a contrary view.

"Today's Desperido reflects the energy you and Ilan brought. Without that spirit, I doubt our growth will be sustained."

"He's right," Elian said. "When word gets out that you two ain't running the show, our protection will fall apart. The cartels, the constables, the Montez Group. They'll make sure this town disappears."

"You gave me new life, boss," Ship chimed in, raising his syneth-manufactured arm. "I won't let you go down there alone."

I was touched. Sort of.

"Thoughts, Ilan?"

He held a new cigar but had yet to light it.

"Vargas said the Jewel was testing our faith. I hang my faith on big guns and speed. We're thirty times faster than humans. We turn people into corpses before they hear us fire. Same can't be said for the rest of you. I don't mean to insult. I'm talking facts."

Yep. That about summed it up.

Our lieutenants bristled, but nobody objected. How could they?

"He's right, my friends. We appreciate your loyalty. We know it's about as unshakeable as those Children of Orpheus. But if the drains are well defended, we have a better chance on our own."

Saul intoned.

"I have no background in these matters, Raul. Yet I might ask a simple question."

"Please do."

"Can you and Ilan run through cages, gates, and solid walls?"

I chuckled at the provocative query, but Moon held a stone face. I conceded the point.

"Unfortunately, Saul, our syneth does not allow us to transmute into anything other than human male form."

"Since we do not know the extent of their defenses," Saul added, "you could potentially kill everyone in your way and still find yourself trapped beneath the town. I'd offer a compromise plan."

It didn't have to cross his lips.

"Ilan and I go in alone but leave a rescue team on standby."

He nodded. "It's practical, allows you to improvise as needed, but includes a failsafe if your strategy goes awry."

"I like it," Genoa said. "We communicated well as a team on the tumbler. We can do it again. The moment you're stuck, we'll make our move."

I liked it too, but not necessarily with the group sitting around my table. These people would fight bravely to their last breath. But that environment called for a different kind of fighter.

"I say we take a break, my friends. The truth is, we were given no timetable to meet Ixoca. We haven't even decided on a day or night strategy. A few more hours of contemplation won't hurt our chance for success."

Soon thereafter, I found myself sitting in the cantina sharing a drink with a fellow veteran of the Swarm war.

# 16

**B**ETT ORTIZ KILLED THE ENEMY in space; I slaughtered them hand to hand. She maneuvered her single-seat Hornet with others to form a web around a Swarm war cruiser; I blasted six-inch holes through enemy armor with a Force Drum. We both worked with teams, but I often went rogue (much more satisfying).

That's how we fought as humans. When I ascended to godhood and faced the Swarm again, my tactics changed. I disclosed none of that as we reminisced about a war that ended twenty standard years ago.

I led with the topic after opening a bottle and pouring each of us a drink. She struck me as a woman who might put aside her animus for a shared experience. I was correct.

"Do you miss it?" I asked.

She tapped the scar next to her prosthetic eye.

"The war? No. But the edge?" She grabbed her drink and swirled it. "I miss waking up to it."

"The rush? The adrenalin?"

She tossed back the liquor and wiped her lips.

"Open my eyes and ask, 'Will I survive the day?' Splash myself with cold water and get on with it."

"I remember countless mornings like that, sans the cold water."

"I figured you SI boys avoided the front lines."

Was she probing?

"I never confirmed my role in the war. You assumed SI."

"Yeah, OK. I see how you work, Raul. Tight to the vest."

I glanced toward the bar, where Lumen mixed drinks, irritated that I stole her new assistant.

"On the contrary, Bett. I'm always transparent, as far as you know." She forced a tight grin at my subtle wit. "We're here now for that very purpose."

"You want something from me."

"Possibly. I'm curious about this morning. Why did you enter the fray on my behalf?"

Bett's guttural laugh felt like mockery.

"You're confused, Raul. I saw a chance to settle an old score. You happened to be Ernie Carbone's latest mark."

"Nobility or loyalty played no role?"

She wagged a finger in my face.

"I'm too much for you. Gimme that fucking bottle."

Naturally, I complied.

"You speak of old scores. Your grievance with me is still fresh. How long should I wait before you decide to settle it?"

She stopped pouring and glared at me with her proper eye.

"If I came here gunning for you, we wouldn't be talking. Unless I was standing over your casket."

"What a pleasant image. As for your issue with Senor Carbone, I get the impression it's about something less specific."

She thought I was a comedian.

"Less. Specific. You might say. Less specific."

"Wish to elaborate?"

"Why do you care?"

"Perhaps I intend to make a job proposal, and perhaps I enjoy transparency in my contractors."

"*Transparency*. Heh. As far as you know. Right?"

She was quite the fun one. I enjoyed verbal jousting.

"Exactly. What was this morning truly all about, my friend?"

The confident grin disappeared when her jaws tightened.

"Sixteen years on the road, Raul. I saw everything. I know how they run the game."

"They?"

"Everyone. Montez. The guild. The continental governments. The cartels." She tapped her noggin. "I know their filthy goddamn secrets. Kept my mouth shut about most."

"Such as?"

Bett hesitated, which struck me as smart. She had to be wondering what I'd do with the information.

"Take Ernie's con. He ain't the only malgado running an overlay manifest on outer range rubes."

"His actions violate Montez and guild rules, but they turn a blind eye. Why?"

"Same reason every train has a hold three."

"*Every train*?"

She sipped her whiskey and stared at the glass.

"Use your head, Raul. There's more profit in hold three than the others combined, but you'll never find the inventory on company records. The trains supply more than half the night market. But when was the last time a constabulary raided hold three?"

"I assume *never* is the correct answer."

"In one." She swigged. "You're a genius."

I brushed off the sarcasm.

"So, everyone has a hand in the money jar."

"Most. The rest of us? Everyday cunts like me? We take what they pay us, or we get clever. Ernie got clever."

"And you don't much care for that kind of clever, I assume?"

She pushed the bottle away. Bett was done drinking for now.

"I'm all for a man making his mark. But shitting on others to do it? There's gotta be a red line, Raul. A hard red line. Otherwise, what in ten hells did any of it matter?"

"The war, you mean?"

"Yeah. The war. We put it on the line to save these people. How we even won, I'll never understand. The Swarm should've taken us down. In one day, it all turned. Half their ships went quiet. Then came The Wave. Never made sense, but we accepted the official line and celebrated a second chance. So did the other thirty-six billion."

A celebration Moon and I made possible. Ah, to hear a few words of thanks. Not the time, unfortunately.

"It was a remarkable turn of events. Humanity on the brink one day, staring at a bright future the next."

"That's how it felt. Until I returned home. Azteca weren't a place I recognized anymore."

"How so?"

She frowned with suspicion.

"You didn't see the changes after The Wave?"

I did, of course, but our actions affected everyone differently.

"You refer to the corruption and the decadence."

She nodded. "It was like the war never happened. Vets were lucky to pick up our old life or start a new one. The shipping companies were the best bet. Lot of ex-Hornets got slotted to run Nav on road trains. Pay weren't great, but the trains had to run, and that was never gonna change."

"You managed for sixteen years."

"Saw the world through the window of my cab. But that weren't all. I'm a sponge, Raul. I look, I listen, I read. And I got the good sense to put that shit together. Then you came along."

"Hmm. Yes. You took the fall for actions beyond your control."

The cantina door swung open, and a gaggle of contractors entered, celebrating their new profits. As the crowd grew, I expected Lumen to demand Bett return to work.

"Don't think so highly of yourself, Raul. Montez wanted me out, so they found an excuse."

"Ah, yes. The vets. A deep betrayal. What is it they have against war veterans, my friend?"

"You're the man with the intel."

"No, no. I left my position many years ago. I'm merely a common man making his way across the desert in search of fun and profit. Why do you believe veterans are being marginalized?"

She raised the brow over her good eye.

"That's a big word for *fucked*. Why, Raul? Depends who you talk to. Most of my old mates think the blinders are on. Nobody wants reminders of the old days."

"And the rest?'

"The paranoid ... Tolan, we were together from boot camp. He says they're pushing us out because we'll be a problem."

"For what?"

"War of independence. He says the hardliners intend to throw off the Collectorate. They want Azteca free and clear."

That Tolan fella either made a lucky guess or had special insight. Either way, he was correct and I wanted to meet him.

"How will the vets pose a problem?"

"We're loyal to the Collectorate. We fought to save it. I got mates on fifteen worlds. We stood up to the Swarm together. The fuck if we'll let these malgados shit on it."

"Makes perfect sense. If a cabal of isolationists or xenophobes wants to break away, they'd diminish the opposition voices ahead of the fight. Doesn't sound overly paranoid, Bett."

"Not when *you* say it, Raul."

I saw an opportunity to make my move.

"The other Aztecans who fought in your unit ... how often do you speak to them?"

"Varies. Tolan? Maybe twice a month. The others not as often. Why does it matter?"

"Well, you said they'd also been pushed out of work. Do you think they might be interested in new opportunities?"

That drew a half-cocked chuckle.

"What ... *here*?"

"As a staging ground. Bett, I'm in need of professional soldiers. Would your mates be interested, or has too much time passed?"

She leaned in. Despite her tone, I knew she was intrigued.

"The fuck are your proposing?"

"A job that pays extraordinarily well."

"Define *well*."

"How much did you earn in a year for Montez?"

"Seventy thousand creds."

"Each of you can make that with a few hours' work."

It was a damn fine offer, but maybe too specific for Bett. She bowed her head.

"Either you're having me on, or you want us to kill people."

"I need your combat training. It's possible you won't have to kill anyone. It's equally as likely you will."

She reached for the bottle and poured.

"Raul, did you hear anything I said today?"

"Yes, and I think this job will be perfect for you and your mates. For one, it involves a cult not unlike the Swarm. Their devotion is absolute, and they're lethal in defense of their faith. Interestingly, they also wear tattoos." I pointed to my neck. "Right here. The shape of a gear. Ever seen it?"

"No, and I reckon you're full of shit."

"Not at all. Ilan and I have been contracted to retrieve a certain object. The group I mentioned stands in our way." True, from a certain point of view. "My own lieutenants are steadfast, but I'd prefer they be led by trained professionals."

"Expendables, you mean."

"Hardly. Bett, I offer an opportunity for you to achieve a small measure of justice against one of the entities involved in this planet's corrupt cycle. A group that I know, for a fact, seeks an independent destiny for Aztecans."

That got her full attention. Whether she believed it ...?

"They have a name?"

"The Children of Orpheus."

"Never heard of them."

"That's their strategy. I'll happily present my evidence and the mission parameters should you agree to join us and bring along a few mates."

She licked her lips after finishing her fourth drink.

"You couldn't get me killed the first time, motherfucker, so you're trying again."

"On the contrary, I'd love for this job to be the maiden voyage of a long, fruitful association. If you don't believe I'm good for it, ask anyone in town how their profits have taken off under my guidance. Oh, wait. You already know. You've been peppering everyone with ten questions from the time you arrived."

I had her there. Bett's curiosity was dangerous, but it played into my hands at the most crucial moment.

"I don't agree to spit until you show me what you got."

"Bett, mission details will have to ..."

"Weapons. I know you have an armory. I want to see it."

A fair request. What good was a professional soldier without the best tools?

"You'll be impressed. It will rekindle fond memories."

"Then let's do it."

She started to slide from the booth.

"One thing, Bett. After you've seen the armory, I'm sure you'll agree to terms. But I'll need you to contact your people at once. We'll open the external comms."

Bett sighed. Apparently, I hit a nerve.

"Yeah. About that. I'm not sure how many I can round up. Most are drunks or too far off their nut. Tolan, I can count on. Maybe Sisal."

"Three professionals plus my best will suffice."

"I'll do what I can ... after I see the armory."

"Away we go."

I signaled Lumen and said we'd return in short order. Her unibrow voiced its singular displeasure. When we entered my bunker, once owned by the young wannabes Moon and I killed, Bett voiced dismay.

OK, so we weren't the best at managing household chores.

Eh.

Her attitude shifted when I led her to the backroom, where our armory consisted of cabinets lined with every type of small arm and military-grade blast rifle of the past two centuries. Ninety-nine percent was banned outside the military and constabulary. When she gathered up her jaw, Bett reverted to gun worshiper. She grabbed at some as if rediscovering her favorite toys.

"How in ten hells did you pull this together? SI?"

That would have required a lengthy dissertation on syneth and its creative properties. Too soon.

"We've worked hard over the years. Ilan and I are prepared for many eventualities."

"What are you doing in this town, Raul?"

"Complete the job, Bett. Earn the answers."

She knew the UNF-issue weapons as if she still wore the uniform.

"I want ten thousand upfront. Each."

"A hard bargain but doable."

She relented. Soon, we returned to the cantina, where Bett showed little interest in serving drinks. She might not have had a job there much longer, but the down payment more than offset it.

Bett convinced Tolan; he arrived in three days. Sisal said no at first before having a change of heart; he arrived in four days.

Moon and I briefed them on the layout but avoided the most critical details. With the parameters in hand, our professionals drew up a plan and trained the militia who they would lead.

On the ninth day, eight of us piled into Bart.

Saul, having been charged to oversee the defense of Desperido, bid farewell in his usual artful style.

From the Nav, I swung around to our three mercenaries plus Elian, Ship, and Genoa.

"When we return, the drinks are on me."

Then I catalyzed the worm drive and punched in coordinates for just north of Todos Santos.

# 17

**M**OON ACCUSED ME OF GOING SOFT. He said I brought in veterans because I feared for our lieutenants. He insisted I had grown too close and lost my objectivity. My response to his shameful opprobrium ended the debate:

"Six guns are better than three, my friend. Big guns are better than small ones. Professionals are better than amateurs."

I was not emotionally compromised, though Theo and his Addis echo concurred with Moon. However, they thought my "attachment" to people I'd known for only ten weeks was admirable. Theo said I was developing into a well-rounded human.

Naturally, I took offense.

*"I served my sentence, Theo. I'm not homo sapiens and have no desire to become one again."*

He responded as one might if I were laying on his office couch.

*"Nor should you, Royal. But we believe your success long-term will be jeopardized by this shallow artifice you present. Humans who are drawn to your initial magnetism and skillset will not linger when they realize you think of them as mere tools."*

*"They're interchangeable, my friend."*

Theo gasped. *"We're appalled at your callous disregard."*

*"I'm appalled at your half-assed attempt to become a therapist. How long before you bill me for the hours?"*

We fought a few more rounds on the eve of our mission. I insisted

Theo not interrupt my thoughts until we returned from Todos Santos. He made a passing comment about my "self-delusion" and retreated into glorious silence.

However, my choice to add fellow ex-soldiers to the lineup introduced a challenge I had overlooked. Elian, Ship, and Genoa felt slighted. Elian spoke to me in confidence moments after we finalized our mission plan.

"Boss, we know this mission is huge. Life-changing. And we don't have a problem with the newbies. But ..."

"Yes, Elian. Speak your mind."

"Don't you trust us?"

I could've resorted to my usual tactic of smooth salesmanship, but damned if Theo's analysis didn't bounce into my thoughts.

"You know *my* true nature, Elian, because I trust *you*. Not everyone would accept me as you did."

He shaded his eyes, perhaps feeling a tad bit ashamed.

"We're honored to work for you. It's just that ... you're putting Bett's crew ahead of us, and you've only known them a few days."

True. Our plan involved stationing the team in two groups. The frontline of Bett "Stopper" Ortiz, Geraldo "Tracer" Tolan, and Iago "Iggy" Sisal would stand guard within sight of the access point. They'd be the first to engage the enemy. Elian, Ship, and Genoa would hide a hundred meters back along a ridgeline. They'd hold the high ground, monitoring the valley outside town and provide rearguard cover. Unless our plan fell apart and turned into an all-out firefight, my lieutenants weren't likely to see much action.

"Elian, how much do you know about what Hornet fighters experienced during the Swarm war?"

"Everything. I've probably seen every vid, studied all the tacticals of High Admiral Aleksanyan's web offensive."

Typical war fanboy.

"But do you know what it was like?"

"I wasn't there. I was too young. I ..."

"The Swarm were relentless and merciless. Humanity won on a

wing and a prayer." Which was more or less true. "Ortiz, Tolan, and Sisal fought a superior enemy in the black of space. Death hunted them, yet they're still here. Who best to handle a worst-case scenario, my friend?"

He accepted my logic. Nice to see good sense prevail.

"And remember, Elian: If the mission falls apart, you three are our last, best hope. I'd say you've been handed a crucial role."

Elian was tasked to operate Bart remotely if we needed an emergency pickup or some overhead strafing, like during our final confrontation with the Horax. I linked Bart's Nav controls to Elian's shiny new pom.

I assumed Elian passed along our conversation to Ship and Genoa, who had been eager to see considerable action. They were upbeat when we made for Todos Santos.

The vets reverted to full-on UNF mode when I placed rifles in their hands and we conducted drills in the desert. Though we didn't provide the symbiotic body armor they used in the war, all three loved the many toys in our armory and appeared eager for action.

They returned to the nicknames used onboard their last assignment together, the UNF warship Icaria. They were now Stopper, Tracer, and Inky. Though I'd given up on most humans, these folks I understood. As many goddamn times as I died on the battlefield ...

"Tracer" Tolan was built like a man who'd never left the service. Forty-five going on twenty-five. A firm beast with a military crew cut and wide eyes always on alert. Did he ever blink? That became the running question. Tracer did little to ingratiate himself at first; my witty retorts blew past him without a response. Bett said he was suspicious of anyone with a sense of humor.

He warmed after three days of training, even shared a few of his conspiracy theories about a scheme to collapse the Collectorate. Though such a plan existed, I doubt it bore any resemblance to the scenarios he concocted. He never mentioned the mysterious Q6.

"Inky" Sisal hadn't maintained his youthful good looks into his late thirties, though he confessed to missing the UNF every day since his honorable discharge. He arrived in town with flowing locks that made me jealous then worried everyone when he refused to touch a drop of liquor. A first day's run in the desert nearabout broke him. The fella hadn't kept in shape. He begged out, yet Tracer talked him into staying.

Inky did, after all, have seventy thousand reasons to hang about. His petite eyes were overshadowed by a somewhat distorted nose. He made the first joke about his quirky face, which opened the door to many others.

At risk of sounding like my *D'ru-shaya*, I analyzed all three for signs of stress that might impair their abilities at gametime. I hoped my assessment of their psychological well-being proved accurate.

Minutes after we departed Desperido and surprised the vets with our illegal worm drive modification, we landed in the hills two kilometers north of the target.

Ten minutes after sunset.

We deployed a pair of sighter drones to scout ahead, attached heat-sensing night goggles, doublechecked comms, verified Elian's remote link to Bart's Nav, and proceeded into the young evening.

We followed the route Horatio Vargas laid out in his message. He knew the surrounding hills well; we couldn't have plotted an easier trek through an otherwise dicey terrain.

The forest was thick with ancient barantha trees – their trunks at least three meters across and their lowest branches of needles ten meters high. The underbrush didn't amount to squat – ground caked by years of barantha needles prevented much growth. That lent itself to excellent cover and wide berths to move between strategic hiding places.

Only problem: A heavy rain pushed through hours before we arrived, turning the needles into a slippery mat. This proved troublesome as we traveled along sharp slopes.

Ship lost his balance and rolled thirty meters before slamming into a trunk. The kid bounced up like a trooper, but he had to be in a mess of pain (at the very least, his ego took a hell of a shot). Fortunately, he hid his discomfort behind those goggles.

"I'm good, boss," he insisted. "I'm good. Seriously. Very good."

He tried hard to cover, but I saw him grab at his hip a few times as we neared the first rendezvous point. I saw no visible evidence of mockery from the veterans, but they certainly must have thought the kid far out of his element. They weren't wrong.

When we reached the ridge from which my lieutenants were to be stationed, I announced:

"Team 2, this is you. Take position. Keep those eyes peeled."

From that vantage, we earned our first clear view of Todos Santos as it stretched from the single entry at the south end, snaking along a hillside north. A few glow lamps cast a soft tint from inside the stone walls. A small ravine separated us, with a stream and one very special drain at the bottom.

"We'll have your backs," Genoa said.

"I know you will, my friends, but let's hope you aren't needed."

Moon and I descended with Bett's crew. The atmosphere changed as we navigated a forty-degree slope and the town gradually rose above us. I hadn't approached an enemy stronghold with a contingent of my peers in two thousand years.

The last time, I ran with the Twenty Talons in black body armor, killing everything in sight with Force Drums. We walked over fields blended with Swarm and Talon corpses. It wasn't a war of choice; circumstance flung me between universes and settled me into a fight I couldn't escape. In time, I embraced that shit. It became my purpose for living. We were brothers and sisters fighting an enemy we'd never defeat in a war rigged against us from the start.

Damn, those were the days: The final years I was human and didn't have to give a spit about the rules.

Kill the bastards. Survive. Kill the bastards.

Alas, the only fair comparison I'd make then and now was that the people in that town wore tattoos on their necks and worshiped a false god. Like the Swarm, these people were trained to kill in the name of their alleged savior; unlike the Swarm, these people didn't arrive in endless waves or bear full-body armor. Some of them were kids dressed like shepherds. I hoped they came to their senses and stayed at home while Moon and I visited their beloved.

The chatter began as we neared the stream.

"Too quiet down here," Bett told her mates. "Don't like it."

"Stopper's right," Tracer whispered to me and Moon. "No MZs, no motion detectors. Too easy."

Our goggles were equipped with excellent scanning tech. Anything manmade between us and the stone walls should have appeared by now. Horatio must have kept his word. However, we weren't close enough yet to track movement inside the hill.

"I've been assured they're not expecting us, Tracer."

Inky, flanking us to Moon's right, replied:

"In other words, we're staring at a clusterfuck."

I had skirted around the facts when laying out this mission. Stopper, Tracer, and Inky were paid to get us in and out alive. They were muscle; our prize wasn't their concern. I made damn sure our lieutenants did not mention the twenty-million-credit payday.

Deceptive, perhaps. But these soldiers understood how to take orders and not ask questions above their pay grade.

"Assume everything," Moon said. "These assholes ain't right. A hundred might be watching behind those walls."

"Correct," I added. "Waiting to spring." I tapped my ear bead. "Team 2, we're ready to enter. Yell at the first sign of movement."

"Gotcha, boss," Ship said, his voice cracking.

That didn't inspire confidence, but Moon and I couldn't wait. Just as we prepared to make a dash across the stream, Bett said:

"You're making a mistake, Raul."

"How so?"

"They won't fight us out here. We'll be too hard to pin down."

"You may be right, but you're not following us inside. Ilan and I will move like cats. A good chance we'll slip past their patrols."

After a pause, all three said:

"What's a cat?"

Oh. Shit. I forgot. This was the only universe where cats didn't exist. These people should've thanked their stars.

"It's small, quiet, but surprisingly troublesome," I said. "We're off, my friends. Hold your ground unless we call for you."

We ran, but nothing that would've impressed a human. The vets didn't need the distraction. We avoided turning into blurs until we entered the sewer drain.

The stream ran low and fast but was littered with rocks. Our goggles helped us dance around them. Water flowing from the drain acted as a tributary which guided us through a jumble of underbrush. The opening was two meters in diameter.

Only when we reached the entrance did our goggles detect heat signatures far inside the hill. I opened my pom and applied the readings against the data we retrieved from Horatio.

They matched.

A straight shot to a T, about seventy meters. Behind the heat signatures? A solid wall of stone. Either the predicted death trap or something special to decipher.

"Ready, my friend?"

"Let's do this, partner."

We slung our rifles and reached for a simpler, quieter weapon.

Our knives were long, thin, and serrated.

We studied our targets, who stood stationary at the junction.

"Go at twenty meters," I whispered.

"On it."

We advanced as advertised. Just like with cats, the two guards would not see us until we pounced and scratched.

But first, we flew. Or so it felt.

I wondered what it must've been like for those two hapless souls, stationed at a dark, miserable post, protecting a creature beyond their understanding.

When did they first detect a disturbance? Did they hear a nonspecific echo of pattering feet but see no silhouettes of an approaching enemy? Did they raise their weapons in abject fear that they had the horrible misfortune of wrong duty, wrong time?

I cherished the thought.

On the bright side, they didn't suffer. We came at them with our blades held in a tight grip, aimed for their necks, piercing through that silly tattoo of the Founders Memorial.

They gurgled and died without protest.

Poor bastards had no idea. Of all the mysteries we faced heading into this mission, my top question remained: Why would these people be fed to the slaughter? If I took Horatio at his word, Ixoca made the call.

False god indeed.

Normally, I hated those assholes. I'd seen a galactic empire wipe out billions in the name of a non-existent deity. In this case, I gleefully put aside my bias.

"Now for the dicey bit," I told Moon.

We flicked on head lamps. A quick glance at the bodies told me Horatio's son avoided a horrible end. So far.

We studied the stone wall, which our tech saw through. Beyond a solid foot of rock, a tunnel led to a descending, winding path.

"It's a door," Moon said. "We need a key, partner."

We shared a smile as I retrieved the marble chip.

The patterns in the stone face matched the chip, but the surface contained just enough striations and indentations to make finding a geometric match difficult.

My ear rang with Bett's voice.

"We have your link, Raul."

I tapped the bead. "Confirmed."

My pom acted as a tether, sending out data that was inaccessible beyond the hillside, giving them a clear view into the drains. Whether they'd be able to follow us beyond the door and down to ... wherever ... remained an open question.

"OK, my friend. Let's find the keyhole."

The door acted like one of those mind-baffling puzzles that

required a person to shift his perspective out of whack in order to see the hidden pattern.

"There."

Moon pointed to a spot right-center. Upon close inspection, I too saw the hexagonal imprint. I pressed the chip into the slot and...

Absolutely nothing happened.

Of course.

I realized my mistake right away: The imprint had a millimeter of wiggle room on all sides. Not a match.

"I get it. Somebody's having a laugh."

Seeing the first hexagon triggered my eyes to see many others, as if they'd been magically disguised.

Eight. Ten. Twenty.

Shit.

"Ixoca is pissing me off."

The chip failed on the first five tries.

"Head's up," Bett said with considerable urgency. "Two signatures on the move."

Good thing for her team. We'd lost track of enemy threats while searching for the keyhole. I confirmed a figure approaching from both directions. They did not move with speed.

"A patrol or a change of the guard. Teams 1 and 2, stand ready."

I tried the seventh, eighth, ninth slots.

Not a damned thing.

"They'll see us in about ten seconds," Moon said. "Let's deal with them first and get back to this door."

It was a tempting proposition.

"You're right. Just one more. And ..."

When I inserted the chip this time, it vanished into the stone, which began to move. It was a pocket door.

"We're in," I announced.

We extinguished our head lamps, but not soon enough.

Green laser bolts chased us from the left and right flanks.

Damned inconvenient.

# 18

WE WERE FAST. BLINK-OF-AN-EYE FAST. But in that tight setting, the perfect ricochets could take us out. Judging from the chaotic dancing of laser bolts off the walls, our enemy also knew this. They fired wildly. So much so, neither Moon nor I got the drop on the shooters.

"In," I shouted.

My partner followed me through the pocket door. We took up a defensive position five meters inside the tunnel and waited for the barrage to cease. If these assholes were dumb enough to pursue, we'd drop them.

When the shooting stopped, I contacted the teams.

"It's a fair bet the town knows we're here. So much for a quiet entry. Raise your game, my friends."

"Do you need to abort?" Bett said.

"Negative. We're pursuing the target. Keep them busy. We'll find out soon enough how long our comms tether will hold. Raul out."

I didn't want anyone following us, but the longer we lingered here, the more dangerous our situation grew outside.

The point became moot when the pocket door slid shut.

Moon asked the obvious first question, to which I answered:

"For now, assume it's on a timer."

"We don't have another key, partner."

"Nope. Only one choice."

We flipped on our head lamps and followed the tunnel. I checked my pom; the tether was holding. For now.

"Excited, my friend?"

"Ask me when we get there."

"*When* being the operative word."

Where the tunnel ended, a winding staircase began. The steps were polished marble, cut to perfection. The solid rock walls, however, showed no such polish. The stairs weren't wide enough to walk two abreast, so I gave Moon the honors.

"If it's a trap with a horribly painful end, you'll have the privilege to die first, my friend."

He moaned as if in distress. I recognized that tone.

"You're not as funny as you think, Royal. Never have been."

I trudged behind. My pom showed these stairs winding in a tight spiral for at least another hundred meters.

"You hurt me, Moon. Genuinely."

"Not in the slightest."

"OK. True. But you don't appreciate my humor because you've endured it too long. Humans are more susceptible to its charms. Except perhaps for Lumen."

He pressed on, silent for a moment until:

"She needs to go, Royal. When we return to town, either she leaves or we kill her."

"I'll take it under advisement, partner. The poor coit has outlived her usefulness, but we wouldn't be here now if she never handed over that truncator. And running the cantina *is* a thankless job."

"None of it will matter after we're paid."

"True. But we have to retrieve the Jewel first, my friend."

We completed ten spirals, with many ahead. My pom completed an analysis of the steps, and its holo confirmed what my eyes suspected.

"Moon. Stop. Look at this."

The staircase top to bottom formed a perfect cylinder. Each spiral declined at the identical slope. The treads and risers never varied in their measurements.

Moon shrugged. "It's impressive."

He sounded underwhelmed, but I reached a logical conclusion.

"Humans didn't construct this. It would've taken years through solid rock. The engineering is too precise, my friend."

"Ixoca?"

"The Jewels terraformed planets. Who would know better?"

Moon pointed to the bottom of the cylinder, where the stairs abruptly ended.

"We'll find out soon enough. Keep moving, Royal."

He gave an order and I complied.

Strange feeling.

Yet that paled against what happened next. The polished treads glowed beneath our feet.

They were pale at first, almost like an optical illusion. After a few more spirals, each tread flashed a soft, hazy blue to the rhythm of our footfalls. I stopped, stomped, skipped, retreated, and doubled my pace. The glows matched every contact.

"Definitely not a human design," I muttered. "But clever."

Soon, the blue flashes came accompanied by soft bell tones. My pom showed five more spirals until we reached the end. Was that where our host awaited us?

Moon raised his hand.

"Don't move!"

He pointed ahead, where just around the bend, blue striations swam along the stone walls, like the reflection of ripples in water. I double-checked my tech.

"No new data. What choice do we have? Onward, my friend."

The effect intoxicated me with a peaceful balm. It produced no sound, and I couldn't determine how it was generated. Did the stone itself have a pulse? I stopped to pursue the theory.

"Hold up, my friend."

I raised my goggles and leaned in to a hair's breadth of the wall.

Then I heard it. Something breathed from within.

What in the ten hells ...?

I opened my eyes to a roomful of desperate voices shouting over each other. Instead of the staircase, I stood alongside Moon on the command bridge of a starship.

Officers scrambled between stations. The forward viewport showed the vessel descending through waves of storm clouds at too sharp an angle. The officers spoke of nonresponsive navigational controls, loss of aft dampening fields, and an explosion in the engine array.

An imperious fellow looked down upon the lower rows of officers. He was easily seven feet tall and presumably the Captain. He surveyed the madness with a calm, cool air. The Captain grabbed nothing for support when the ship buckled from turbulence.

I didn't feel shaking beneath my feet, nor did the Captain appear to notice our sudden arrival.

However, someone else saw us.

He entered the bridge behind the Captain, a man in the same uniform but with less stripes. His eyes twinkled with the blue of the staircase. He approached us like a rabid damn animal.

"Had to be done," he said. "You understand. Had to be done."

He shook me by the shoulders, though I didn't feel shaken.

"What had to be done?" I asked, but no sound crossed my lips.

"There." He pointed to the forward viewport, where the planet rose in a damn hurry. "See it."

"See what?"

"See it. No. Not there." He pointed upward. "*There!*"

My focus narrowed. Above the window that foretold approaching disaster, I saw a logo and a name.

*S.P.S. Carrier Orpheus.*

I nudged Moon and pointed to the revelation.

"How?" My partner said, as lost in the moment as me.

We were there, but not there.

A bubble? A memory? A simulation?

Answers had to wait.

The blink of an eye returned us to the staircase. The blue striations disappeared, leaving only the glowing steps beneath us.

"Didn't see that coming, my friend."

"The Orpheus crash?" Moon asked.

"For the sake of argument, I'll say yes. Think maybe somebody's trying to teach us a little history."

"That lunatic with the blue eyes was not subtle."

"No. What 'had to be done'? Bring down the Ark Carrier? I for one am intrigued to continue."

So we did but with a more cautious pace.

Two spirals shy of the bottom, the light show returned.

"OK then. Another trip through time?"

We touched the glowing walls and reappeared elsewhere.

Again, the room was large and the voices every bit as chaotic. People in business suits yelled over each other from across a long table. Someone pounded a gavel.

And …

*Wait.* The perspective wasn't my own this time. I tried but failed to find Moon. Was he present?

I vaguely heard someone's thoughts, like echoes in my own brain. They were distressed and wanted the hell out of there.

"Madame President." A woman stood at the table's far end. "Your proposal for the appropriations bill is a non-starter. My people will not support these cuts."

To which a man nearer to my end replied:

"The President is making the only sensible move to keep the interstellar customs tax in line with the Constitution."

Then the voices blurred, but I had enough evidence to know this place. I damn sure hadn't been taken back eleven hundred years. This was Amity Station, home of the Interstellar Congress and the President's office.

The perspective changed. The eyes through which I was forced to see shifted to the current Collectorate President Kara Aleksanyan. Though only two years older than the last time we met in person, she seemed like a woman burdened with too much baggage.

She pounded the gavel again.

"We're making no progress. We'll resume in the morning, when I hope cooler heads prevail."

A man with thick shoulders and a beefy neck whispered in her ear. I recognized this fellow.

Ah, yes. Leonard. The President's personal chief of security and our contact while in her service.

The President nodded toward me, and I followed her out a rear exit along with Leonard. But who was I? Perhaps more important: Why was I seeing this at all?

My host (for lack of a better term) followed the President and Leonard down a short corridor and into her private office.

"That was a disaster," the President said. "Again. Is it my imagination, or is the Cabinet more hostile by the day?"

"It's about appearances, Madame President," said my host, a man with a calming voice. "They're feeling different pressures back home. They take it out on you."

"They're supposed to be my allies, Kai."

"Give them time. I recommend postponing the next assembly for three days. A cooling off period."

President Aleksanyan delivered a cynical gaze, an expression I recalled from my brief encounters with Kara.

"If you weren't my Chief of Staff, I'd say you want me to fail. Give these people more time to sharpen their knives? No. Tomorrow."

"Very well, Madame President."

Kara fell into a cushy chair behind a surprisingly unimpressive and largely barren desk.

"Leonard, have you confirmed the intel from our friends?"

He leaned in, settling his arms on her desk.

"It's worse than we feared. Our friends were right about Q6."

*Our friends.* Was that code for me and Moon?

Kara bowed her head and sighed.

"Tell me."

"We don't have an identity, but my sources confirm Q6 is known on at least ten worlds. He has many buffers, but his network does pose a threat. As we suspected, he's working primarily through the shipping guilds. They'll be the focal point when he delivers the call to action."

"Which will be what?"

"Strikes."

Kara pulled a digipipe from her breast pocket, tapped it, and pulled on the leaf inside.

"Nothing would undermine our credibility more than a trade stoppage. I won't stand for it, Leonard. Can our friends help?"

"I believe so, though they might not trust us. If they've been following the news from Qasi Ransome, our friends may suspect a trap to silence them."

"Understandable. We did contemplate it, after all."

Oh, how gracious, Kara. We eliminate threats to your power, provide golden intel, and you consider killing us. Lovely.

She asked: "Have you prioritized potential targets?"

Leonard nodded. "I have. The confluence on Azteca is the most pressing. My sources believe the flashpoint will happen there. When and where? Uncertain."

"Do we have specific targets?"

"My contacts are compiling names. If our friends are amenable, we can act within the month."

She leaned back in her chair and swiveled.

"You believe this is more pressing than that sore spot on Inuit?"

"I do, Madame President. It's far more advanced."

Kara exhaled a thin stream of white smoke.

"At least our friends won't have to leave their neighborhood."

"True. But I must remind you, it will be a temporary salve. We can't silence the threat on Azteca without a full-scale assault."

Kara motioned the Chief of Staff to her side. Suddenly, I stood within a meter of the woman for whom I secretly worked.

"If it buys a few months, I'll take it. Kai, I'd like you to arrange the drop this time. Leonard needs to focus on intel."

"Of course, Madame President. I'll take care of it as soon as I have the data."

Just as the moment grew juiciest, I felt a tug and then a flash. For an instant, I expected to blink and return to the staircase. Instead, a second flash carried me to a new location.

I walked the tight corridor of a spaceship through another set of eyes. A man approached in a blue/black uniform. He carried himself as military, but he wasn't. How did I know this?

"Captain, the strike team is landing now."

"Very good," my host said. "I want the matter executed with haste. We have ten minutes until the orbital net exposes our presence."

"Col. Raeger is the best, sir. If it's breathing, he'll kill it."

Together they walked onto the bridge. It was compact. Only three officers. Similar to the UNF warship configuration but with a few variations. Interesting. They didn't wear the UNF stars, and their chest medals were circular. They ...

Shit.

Special Intelligence.

Had to be.

"Give me visual," the Captain said from his chair.

The holo showed a team of heavily armed men in full body armor scattering amid the ruins of ...

*The Fort of Inarra.* Our home of nineteen years. Not a sweet one, but it got us through.

Now, I had a timeline – to the minute.

I also knew what came next.

Moon and I had watched the assault on our home from Desperido by way of our poms. We allowed the defense perimeter to act according to its design protocol.

It exploded to life and trapped those poor sods within a web of lightning. Their screams mortified the Captain and his bridge officers. He shouted for Col. Raeger to abort the mission.

Never had a chance.

Every human inside the fort roasted to death.

The bridge fell silent until the comms officer announced:

"No life signs, Captain."

The Captain sounded broken.

"How many did we lose, Lieutenant?"

"Twenty."

"Commander Turin. Your recommendation?"

The officer who first informed the Captain of the landing gazed in horror. I saw his little mind working to salvage the moment.

"Captain, we can't leave evidence. The shuttle, the bodies."

"Agreed, Commander. Lt. Suh, engage worm. Bring us in close enough for an immediate strike. Commander, load the package. Scorched earth."

"Yes, Captain."

The ship jumped to worm. Just as I remembered it, the vessel exited the aperture above the fort and unloaded its heavy guns on the site. Nothing left behind but shrapnel and ash.

"He'll pay for this," the Captain muttered.

He pounded his chair's armrest.

A white flash yanked me away.

My eyes opened to the staircase; Moon stared back at me.

I gathered my thoughts.

"Were you there? Did you see it, my friend?"

"Yes, Royal. The President. The fort. I was inside other minds."

"The Prez's Chief of Staff. An SI Captain."

"SI destroyed our fort. Was it ...?"

I tried to piece the pronouns together until they made sense.

"Her Chief of Staff must've been the traitor. A man named Kai. We always suspected it had to be someone close to the Prez. And the Captain said, '*He'll* pay for this.'"

"Q6? You think he's Q6?"

I chose instinct over the improbable.

"No. An operative, perhaps. A double agent. But I wonder if ..."

A sudden burst of warm air rushed past us.

Behind it, a voice filled the staircase. Disembodied but familiar. An older man? A woman?

"My eyes are many," it said. "My eyes have turned to you. Join me that we may understand each other."

I could well imagine ordinary humans pissing their pants about now. The technology was outstanding and the special effects mesmerizing. Fortunately, we'd seen nearabout every miracle imaginable.

Eh. We shrugged and agreed to descend.

"Two more spirals," Moon said.

"I have a good feeling, my friend. This will not be a letdown."

"You're too much of an optimist, Royal. It bit you in the ass before. Better hope it doesn't again."

Fair point. My partner had made several lately.

We descended the last two spirals with haste. The final few steps did not glow beneath our feet. We entered a flat, dark chamber.

"Huh. This is ... underwhelming."

"There," Moon pointed. "I see something."

Indeed, a faint blue light drew us forward ...

To the edge of a cliff.

No, not a cliff.

A shaft. Cylindrical.

Tiny blue sparkles flickered from the walls like jewels. I had no sense of the bottom, so I checked my pom.

Two readings surprised me: The relay to the outside world remained intact. If they weren't under assault, my teams at least knew we had traveled deep into the planet. According to the data, this shaft burrowed down another three hundred meters.

"Not helpful," I mumbled, wondering if anyone might hear.

Apparently, something did.

"Jump."
It was the same older voice, accompanied by a warm breeze.
"Jump now, or you will never know the truth."

# 19

**M**OON'S PREDICTABLE RESPONSE amused me. "We just got bit in the ass."

It was hard to argue the point, but I tried.

"Horatio said Ixoca would test our faith. I believe he's doing just that. He wants us to take a literal leap of faith, my friend."

Moon glanced behind to the dark chamber.

"Jump three hundred meters? Royal, even if our syneth can withstand the fall, look at the data. There's no way out."

"No, there isn't. This may very well be the end for us. Lured by shiny things and trapped forever. Ah, remember the days when we too could toy with the universe?"

Moon closed his pom and stowed it.

"You're going to jump. Aren't you?"

I planted my feet firmly on the edge, my toes hanging over.

"If this is how we claim the future ... yes. You feel it, Moon. The moment we retreat and climb those stairs, we're done. We'll break the timeline. Nothing we planned will come to pass. This, my friend, is our crossroad."

"Or our grave."

I stowed my pom as well.

"Those flashes from the past weren't meant as trinkets to lure us to our doom. It's bait, no doubt. But also a demonstration of the Jewel's power. It chose us, Moon." I chuckled. "Also, if you'd like, I can hold your hand on the way down."

He scoffed. "You're an asshole, Royal. From the first day we met."

"True, but a good asshole. A loyal and devoted friend. Yes?"

"Most of the time. If you're sure ..."

"Faith, my friend."

I could have called upon Theo to regulate my syneth core during the jump, but I had told the psychobabbling prick to go silent until the mission concluded.

Yeah, no. I didn't need him. Honestly, I was surprised he hadn't yet intervened since his own ass was also on the line.

"Think of it like the old days, Moon. Flying between stars in a matter of seconds. A thought, a twist, and there we were. Thousands of light-years away. Easy peasy."

Moon smiled at the memory of our golden age.

I put one foot in front of the other and fell.

It was a beautiful goddamn sensation. The sparkles whooshed past like I was crisscrossing the stars again.

I never looked down. If this was the end, I wanted it to be sudden and inexplicable.

Instead, I landed like a feather. Moon did, too, a second later.

However, the shock of a gentle landing didn't paralyze our instincts. We drew our weapons.

Blue light consumed us. My optical sensors adapted until the brightness receded to reveal a ribbed structure wrapping around the base of the shaft. Cartilage and tendons filled the gaps, where blue striations channeled in vertical lanes between the bones. We stood on a firm mattress of taut muscles.

Horatio's words flashed before my eyes:

*"If you succeed, you will see his heart."*

I never took that statement literally.

"Guess where we are, my friend?"

"Unless there's a hidden door, Royal? Trapped."

"Who knows? We already passed through one."

Hidden doors, like secret lairs, excited me.

Moon asked, "What now? We took his leap of faith."

"Perhaps lower our weapons. Show a tad more respect for the old fella. We're inside his heart, after all."

We stowed our rifles; seconds later, the cartilaginous striations intensified. A warm rush of air surrounded us. The older, neutral voice filled the chamber.

"It is less a heart than a vessel," the Jewel said. "I have many."

A topographical holo of Azteca hovered above us. It highlighted subterranean cylinders like this one. They appeared to be spaced equidistant across the planet.

"How many, Ixoca?"

"Three thousand."

"And their purpose?"

"Creation."

"The mechanism for terraforming?"

"Yes. We constructed them half a million years before the arrival of homo sapiens. My brethren appointed me to stay behind and oversee this world's transformation."

I thought it best not to jump ahead with questions of present-day urgency. Our host seemed to enjoy teaching history. Time to indulge the instructor.

"You stayed behind after the job was finished?"

"No. I joined my brethren in the dark reaches of space to build the transit network."

"The Fulcrum?"

A holo of the wormhole tunnels that connected forty star systems replaced Azteca.

"When we finished our work, my brethren chose to travel. They journeyed through the interstitial spaces between universes and returned for the culmination of prophecy."

"Ah. The end of Hiebimini and its redesign as Aeterna."

"Yes. I and one other did not join the great journey. I settled here and waited for humanity's interstellar migration."

"The other? Was he the one who visited Earth and triggered the rise of the human race?"

"He was."

"Most of your kind now live quietly beneath Aeterna. Yes?"

"They do."

A holo of the immortals' home world replaced The Fulcrum.

"The human migration finished a thousand years ago. Why did you remain on Azteca?"

No answer.

The holo vanished.

Did I ask the wrong question? It seemed the logical follow-up.

"The answer is complicated, Raul Torreta."

The voice changed. Younger, sharper, and entirely feminine.

Also in the chamber with us.

The blue striations released a fine mist of sparkles which pixelated into the vague form of a human. A lovely effect! The new manifestation of Ixoca circled us while a channel of sparkles from the ribbed wall infused it with energy.

"Our creators, the J'Hai, designed my kind to improve their lives and guide them across the stars. We failed in that charge. We lit out upon the galaxy determined to justify our existence. We saw potential in the emerging creatures who would become homo sapiens. We gifted humans a sector of the galaxy when they came of age."

Her explanation to that point offered no great surprise. Moon and I observed the moment when a Jewel entered the mind of Earth's first Chancellor.

"I reckon that was an ambitious and noble goal, Ixoca. How many planets did your people terraform?"

"Twenty-three of the forty, although we made environmental adjustments on many more."

"Ah. Tweaks to suit humans. Yes?"

The blue pixelated shape turned red. Its shoulders stiffened and its features flattened.

"Customized so each planet would stand apart." The man's voice was stiff and all business. "Each one tailored to the needs we projected based on our study of long-term causality."

"Nice. *Causality*. One of my favorite words. Agree, Ilan?"

He sighed. "*The* favorite."

"So, let's get back to you, Ixoca. All these worlds were custom designed, and you had the major hand in Azteca. In a sense, you're this planet's creator. Its veritable God."

The red man stopped circling, pivoted to us, and revealed a single human eye amid the pixels.

"No one ever used that word in my presence. Even the humans who speak to me won't bring themselves to say it."

"Frustrating, isn't it? Ilan and I understand. Respect for gods is in short supply. Tell us: Why did you remain on Azteca after the humans colonized?"

Ixoca resumed his circular pacing.

"I chose a destiny apart from my brethren. They wished to explore. I preferred to evolve. My design was incomplete. I wanted to become much more."

I snapped my fingers.

"We're right there with you, my friend! Evolve and ascend. Nice. Judging from that first little flashback, you evolved before humans arrived. You were able to watch the Orpheus crash from inside the Ark Carrier. Am I right?"

Ixoca grew a second eye, lips and a rib cage inside the pixelation. Humans might've found the sight unnerving, but I was fascinated for the final reveal.

"Chancellor scientists had traveled here for a century and mapped my world. Established footholds for cities. I watched and listened. I came to despise them. They did not deserve my gift."

The businesslike tone added an edge of resentment.

"How so, Ixoca?"

"The Chancellors sought only to exploit this planet for its mineral wealth. They intended to dump an inferior class of humans here. Purifying Earth, they called it. I would not allow them to populate my planet with their trash. By the time their first colony ship arrived – the Ark Carrier Orpheus – I had made the greatest evolutionary breakthrough in the Jewel design. I split my core matrix into separate but equal parts. I entered the Orpheus as it orbited Azteca. I created a hazard within the engine array. When Orpheus descended, the engines exploded. The ship tore itself apart."

Ixoca's eyes ballooned into bloodshot terror as he shouted:

"It had to be done!"

That explosion chilled me just a nudge. I shared an uneasy glance with my partner. Moon knew: We were facing a full-on megalomaniac.

Very nice.

"So, it was you all along. I doubt your Children know the truth."

Ixoca pulled himself together, color-shifted to blue, and reasserted a feminine presence.

"What they know, Raul, is that I saved them from certain oblivion. For that, they have always been grateful."

"OK. From villain to savior in one fell swoop. Explain."

"I manufactured the virus that eliminated most crash survivors. It was spreading across my planet and would have killed all others, leaving Azteca pristine."

"What changed?"

"As the number of survivors dwindled, my new matrix entered their minds. I wanted to retain their last thoughts for my memories."

I saw the next bit coming from a light-year away.

"Huh. They weren't the people you expected, were they? Not trash. Not inferior to Chancellors. And not interested in exploiting Azteca."

"No. They had been stripped of their homes. They sought only to start new lives and hold on to the legacies of their ancestors. They were terrified. They grieved for their children. Their journey had come to naught."

I finished the narrative for her.

"So, you reversed course. Everyone whose mind you touched, you made immune to the virus."

"I did."

"And you made sure they knew who was responsible. Gratitude wasn't enough. You wanted a legion of followers."

Ixoca created a fist out of the pixelation.

"Why not? I gave them my world. I made them special among the millions who followed. All I asked in return was dedication toward a higher goal. As I continued to evolve, I saw a path for this planet and its people to rise above all others."

That gave me pause.

"Heard that bit before. Conquest on your mind, Ixoca?"

"No. Only triumph over the mundane."

"How'd that work out?"

The blue body, now seventy-five percent formed, added a pair of supple breasts, a delightful belly button, and a vagina.

"The Chancellors ruled over the immigrants for a thousand years. My Children were incapable of changing their destiny."

"Then the Chancellors fell thirty-two years ago. You've been gaming the system ever since. Preparing these people. Yes?"

She tilted her head to acknowledge my accuracy.

"Long ago, I planted pieces of myself in my Children. After the fall of the Chancellory, I expanded my eyes and ears. When The Wave changed the face of reality, I found new motivation in the people. They believe in a separate destiny for Azteca. They actively work on my behalf, here and throughout the Collectorate."

"You assign them duties?"

"A few. Yes. My generals."

"Horatio Vargas, for example?"

"Yes."

"The people of Todos Santos?"

She shook her head.

"Guardians. They will fight when called upon."

"You call them guardians. I call them assassins. A more accurate term. Yes?"

"From a certain point of view."

I was warming up to this wild coit. Then again, what wasn't to love about a true agent of chaos?

"OK then. That brings us to the present, my friend. You showed us the President. We know where her loyalty lies. You showed us the attack on the Fort of Inarra. We know who's working against her. A demonstration of your many eyes, I presume?"

She smiled for the first time.

"Many and well hidden."

"Is their assessment correct? Azteca will be the flashpoint for the uprising led by this person codenamed Q6?"

Ixoca's full chest and abdomen formed. Only one arm and the back remained pixelated.

"The President will contact you soon to take out targets on this planet. They are unconvinced you were killed in the assault on Inarra."

"So, that was Q6's plan? Eliminate us before we became a greater threat?"

Ixoca winked.

"Not exactly."

"We're listening, my friend."

She cupped her hands over her chest.

"My many eyes focused on you the day you entered Desperido."

Moon shot me a hard look of recognition.

Shit. Why didn't I make the connection sooner?

"Lumen."

Ixoca nodded. "She isn't aware of me. Many of my Children are passive observers. I studied you. I saw how you destroyed her son, who was both guardian and observer. It's painful to watch the death of a child. I ordered Horatio to introduce us and make an offer."

I knew the answer to my next question but asked it as a courtesy.

"Why?"

"Because you and I are perfect for each other. Because you will help me lead the revolution."

Yep.

"You know what we are. Don't you?"

Ixoca grinned like one of those cats that didn't exist in this universe.

"I know what you were. I know what you seek. Our interests are aligned, Raul Torreta and Ilan Natchez."

"Are they?"

"Complementary."

"Eh. We seek to build a criminal empire like nothing in human history. You want Aztecans to break free from the Collectorate and reach some grand destiny. The rule of law means nothing to us, and we'll kill anyone who gets in our way. That might help your little rebellion, but we'll stand at cross purposes before long."

"I disagree," said the suddenly male Ixoca. His spine set in place, and skin rolled over the shoulder blades. "I possess the power and contacts you will need to establish your empire in exchange for your assistance to end the Collectorate."

Yep. Definitely a megalomaniac. Very exciting.

"You have eyes, but that doesn't prove power."

He imitated my signature finger wag to silence the audience.

"Ixoca is the name these people chose for me. But it is not my name. The J'Hai assigned identities when they created the Jewels of Eternity. I was one of four thousand. The J'Hai honored me with a name. I honor them always."

The last pixelation vanished. I stared at a fully constructed human. Naked, hairless, tall, muscular, bearing the curves and sleekness of an athletic, sexual, and intellectual creature. I admired its evolved gender-free perfection. Then the Jewel threw me totally off my game.

"The J'Hai named me Q6."

Yeah, no.

Moon didn't believe it either.

"Come again?"

## 20

**M**OMENTS OF CLARITY ALWAYS snuck up on me. Just as I thought the universe had nothing new to hurl my way, along came a lives-changing surprise. My jaw hung limp as I asked the obvious (and somewhat redundant) question:

"You're Q6?"

The Jewel tilted his head. Or hers.

"So named for three million years, Raul."

Moon interjected for the first time in our dialogue.

"You're behind the conspiracy against the Collectorate? The one overseeing a network on several planets? That's you?"

"Indirectly, Ilan."

"What in ten hells do you mean?"

Q6 gazed above our heads, where dozens of holographs hovered. We saw people from different worlds talking over each other. Meeting in small rooms. Whispering in corners. The words meant little in this jumbled context until I realized a common theme.

In every holo, we saw the crowd through one person's point of view, same as the President's chief of staff on Amity Station and the SI Captain above our dearly departed home.

The Jewel's many eyes.

"In every conversation you see here," it said, "Q6 is invoked at least once. When the code name for their leader spreads, momentum grows. His identity is secret. No one has seen Q6, but they know he lives."

Oh, this was too good!

"There's no such person. He's a legend you created."

"Very good, Raul. Those who whisper my true name believe in Q6 because ..."

"You convinced them yourself."

Q6 wiped away the holos. I knew that smirk of victory quite well.

"I have direct dialogue with my generals. The rest hear my name in their dreams but are sure it came out of conversations with others of like mind. Q6 is the title of a song whose lyrics cannot be shaken once heard. It catalyzes the restless, propels the persistent, and redirects the uncommitted. It's the power of legend."

I was almost speechless.

"Call me impressed, my friend."

"From this moment forward, you will call me Ixoca. That is the name my people know me by, and it must remain so. Other than my brethren, you two are the only ones in Creation who know my true identity."

I nudged Moon.

"Now we come to it. The hour of judgment."

Moon nodded his understanding of our predicament.

"We make a deal with Ixoca, or he kills us."

Our host resumed his pacing with a loud, self-satisfied sigh.

"No one or nothing will die in this place," Ixoca said. "My heart is hallowed ground. We will make a pact and work in league toward the futures we desire. You have a quality I need, and I can offer what you require most."

"Oh, yeah? You can fulfill the top item on our wish list?"

Ixoca crossed hands over its chest.

"Top ten. Top hundred. Name them."

And they called me arrogant! OK, I took the bait.

"Try this on for size, Ixoca: An army of professional killers. Aztecans for a start, but I want a strong interstellar blend. Let's say a dozen worlds. I want the credits to pay them and off-book ships to fly them wherever we intend to plant roots."

Ixoca massaged his chin and contemplated my request.

"How many assassins would you prefer at a minimum?"

I turned to Moon.

"What do you think, my friend?"

His slitted eyes said he didn't know whether we were seriously negotiating or playing a game to buy time.

"We can't make a dent in our goals without an army of hundreds."

"Agreed. There you have it, Ixoca. How about a lowball number to kick things off? Let's say two fifty."

Either the Jewel was a better salesman than I or he was playing one hell of a con. He didn't hesitate.

"I'll do better, Raul. I guarantee five hundred within six months. My eyes extend inside certain cartels and roam on the fringes of others. The ships will be simpler to acquire. An exclusive branch of the night market already exists for special clients."

"Sounds like a dream. What's the price stamp?"

"One hundred million credits."

Moon and I chuckled.

"In six months? How you see that happening, my friend?"

"I'll order Horatio to pay you half his promised twenty million, with the remainder contingent on my satisfaction."

"Huh. Satisfaction of what?"

"Your services rendered, of course. You'll be completing a series of jobs at my request, not to mention what President Aleksanyan will pay after your next mission on her behalf. Given the likely nature of her targets, you should profit another ten million."

I thought of telling him that particular gravy train would end later this year. No. Too soon.

"You have an inkling as to these targets?"

"As you saw earlier, the President's paranoia is focused on Azteca. She will likely ask you to kill individuals whose interests align with my own. You will complete those jobs."

"Slow it down, Master Jewel. You *want* us to sabotage your work?"

"Losses of a few eyes will hurt, but their deaths will galvanize the movement among my people and our allies."

Moon entered the fray.

"What if we're told to take out Horatio Vargas?"

I expected concern, but Ixoca didn't appear to roll that way.

"His loss would be felt, but he's not my only general. It's more important the President and her allies believe they're making progress. Our people will be in place for the reckoning."

Ixoca sounded less like an ancient god and more like a crime lord. Definitely a kindred spirit. There was just one little catch.

"You won't be satisfied if we leave here with a handshake and a gentlemen's agreement. What are your terms?"

"Correct. First, I ask you to acknowledge your true identities, as I have done. Royal and Moon."

What was fair was fair.

"How did you know?"

"For years, I trained my many eyes on learning all I might about The Wave. It unveiled a reality hidden to everyone – including me. For countless humans, it redefined the meaning of life. It accelerated a spirit of independence. One of my generals – you saw him order the destruction of your fort – joined Special Intelligence years ago. Under my guidance, he found the classified records of what happened nineteen years ago on a distant asteroid. In the final moments of that event, after you initiated The Wave and annihilated half the Swarm fleet, you were consumed in fire. I assume you were confronted by a stronger force."

OK then. The jig was up.

"We knew what we were doing."

"You were gods. You killed billions yet saved as many. How did you save yourselves?"

Revealing our knowledge of the future timeline seemed like too big of a giveaway.

"We were exiled, Ixoca. We chose to make the most of what we had. How did you connect the dots to Raul and Ilan?"

Our host maintained that shit-eating grin which, to be fair, was a mere reflection of my own.

"My eyes said you were not human. That narrowed the possibilities. Then I considered your aliases. In the old Earth tongues, Raul meant *wolf*. Ilan meant *serpent*. Eyewitness reports from the incident on the asteroid said you proclaimed yourselves the Wolf and the Serpent. They said you wore tattoos befitting of each. Need I go on?"

The grand finale of our old life. What memories. At least Ixoca acknowledged the good we did. Better than humans ever would.

"Well done. I am Royal. He is Moon. But from now on, you'll have to call us Raul and Ilan, for that is how *our* people know us."

Fair's fair. Yes?

Ixoca stretched out a hand, which I accepted. He held a firm grip but otherwise felt like it belonged to an ordinary human. Moon also shook, though the skepticism poured through his narrow eyes.

"Excellent," the Jewel said. "We now bear each other's secrets. I will demand no more of your story. If you agree to my final condition, we will work together to fulfill our disparate goals. You will help me establish the conditions necessary for Azteca to break free of the Collectorate, and I will help you deliver a scourge across the sector to regain your lost glory."

I pivoted to Moon. Was he sold?

"Thoughts, my friend?"

All our dreams stood on the edge of fruition or oblivion.

"I want to know Ixoca's final condition," Moon said. "If it's fair, I'm in all the way."

The alternative was certain death, so the choice wasn't hard.

"You heard him, Ixoca. Let's have it."

The Jewel pointed to the ribbed structure.

"This is but one of many hearts, all beneath the surface. I want to walk on Azteca. I want to feel the soil beneath my feet. I want to experience the sun's heat against my skin. What better way than inside the bodies of fellow gods?"

From the moment we received the invitation, I suspected what the Jewel wanted from us. I also knew it might be dangerous for all concerned. Yet some damn fine potential! Our syneth reserves depleted, our *D'ru-shayas* less useful than ever. If we harnessed the Jewels' power to terraform planets – even in miniature – what magic could we weave?

Holy. Shit.

Moon spoke for me.

"You want to break off pieces of yourself in us. We're to become your eyes."

The cartilaginous striations intensified as if pumping blood to a heart that beat out of control. Ixoca wagged a finger.

"A piece of me? No. That I reserve for humans. It's all they can handle. I propose a merger. The essence of my core matrix will integrate with the organic technology that sustains you."

"It's called syneth," Moon said.

"You shapeshift and create complex objects. Yes?"

"We do."

I saw exhilaration and relief in the Jewel's face.

"Perfect. When we join, your ability to create and transform will grow exponentially. Your eyes will see the Collectorate as mine do. All my children will become your children. You will follow the President as her Chief of Staff. You will carry out missions through Special Intelligence. You will associate with the most powerful men and women on this planet. And none will ever know."

No amount of credits could buy what Ixoca offered. Moon and I were never going to recapture our godhood in the truest sense, but this was a gorgeous step in the right direction.

*Father and Mother* must have seen the continuum before spitting us out on this planet. It knew we'd reach this moment. Now, all we had to do was accept, and our timeline would hold.

Theo had other ideas, of course.

*"Royal, if you allow this creature to infect your body, it will come for us."*

*"And if I don't, Theo? I die. You die. We discussed this."*

*"Please, Royal. We beg of you. We'll be stronger partners in the future. Addis is terrified. She's weak. Her defenses will not last."*

Now, it was my turn to play therapist.

Yeah, no.

*"Wall yourself off, Theo. Tell Addis to do the same. Hide in the deepest, darkest corner and hope the invader doesn't see you."*

*"It won't be enough. You're a monster, Royal. Remember all the centuries we served you and Moon. If you cast us off now ..."*

I'd always been a selfish prick. My adoptive family taught me the tricks of the trade when I was a child. Now, I was too old to change my ways.

*"Sorry, Theo. You'll have to fend for yourself. You know your mission. We'll speak again soon, my friend."*

*"No! Royal, don't you ...!"*

On he rambled. I brushed him aside and focused on my next life.

"Tell us what to do, Ixoca."

"Come." The Jewel directed us to the wall, where we flanked him. "I will return to the heart and reemerge inside you. Place your hands on the ribs and close off all thoughts of resistance. I must be allowed to enter freely."

"How will we know the merger is successful?"

"At first, little should change. I will speak to you as I did before taking a human shape. The rest will happen over the next hours and days, as our integration finalizes. I must learn your syneth matrix, as it must learn my core. But you will have immediate access to a Jewel's greatest talent: The ability to see life at the cellular level and alter it to suit your needs."

"Fascinating. Good with this, partner?"

Moon allowed a twinkle to break through those skeptical eyes.

"Will the merger help us get out of here?"

"You'll see. Now, your people are encountering difficulties on the surface. Time is short. So, if you please, grab here and there."

We positioned our hands high against the ribs and stood back, our feet spread. When Ixoca was satisfied, he began to disappear into the striations, his body reversing course into tiny streams of sparkles.

As he vanished, I felt an electric vibration rush through my hands, scamper up my arms, and chase the corners of my syneth.

Theo did not protest; I assumed he followed my advice and hid.

Though my so-called heart said I experienced a transformative moment, little else registered a genuine change. My internal temperature briefly fluctuated between warm and cold. It felt like walking in wet sand at the ocean's edge. Each time a wave rolled up, my feet tickled.

Then it ended. The ribs went dark; the striations slowed.

"We're together," Ixoca said on a breeze. "Lower your arms and study your palms."

The skin moved, as if the syneth weren't able to decide what image to create. Bright blue globules rippled just underneath.

"The process of integration has begun," he continued. "Our cores are learning each other. I won't have to explain further. Once the merger is complete, *you* will see the answers, hear the songs, and embrace the chaos of an unprecedented future."

"How do you feel?" I asked Moon.

"The same but new, partner."

"Good. Whatever comes next, one thing ain't gonna change. It's you and me, my friend. Always."

That's how our story had to end.

We lived together. We died together. Now, with a Jewel in tow.

"If you please," Ixoca said. "Stand in the center of the heart. It's time for you to return. They badly need your help."

"How do we ...?"

The muscular floor cut off Moon's question when it dislodged from the cylindrical structure and ascended. Above us, the striations lit up like the brightest night sky. A map to the heavens.

This Jewel knew how to impress gods.

"Not bad, Ixoca," I said. "Not goddamn bad at all."

# 21

**I**XOCA SAID THE CHANGES would be gradual, but the visible spectrum altered right away. I adjusted my optical sensors and saw colors deeper, richer, and layered like nothing since the glory days. My eyes penetrated the blue sparkles along the shaft's walls through to their perpetual energy source. I detected its molecular structure. Given time, I'd translate it into practical uses and command my syneth to replicate it.

"You see the difference?" I asked Moon.

He smiled like a little boy.

"I haven't felt this way since ..."

Moon fell into a silent reverie. I understood. Our previous lives had always focused on becoming more and better. Since the exile, we'd fallen notches closer to human beings.

Finally, a course correction.

"Doubt we'll have need of these." I grabbed the night goggles wrapped around my neck. "When we reach the top, whatcha say we go au naturel?"

"I'm with you, partner."

Our lift carried us past the intersection with the staircase.

"Looks like there's a faster way out, my friend."

I retrieved my pom and opened the comm to our teams. The relay remained intact and allowed me to see combat status. The initial schematic showed all six were still alive but fully engaged with the enemy. I opened the channel.

"Stopper, we're on our way out. What's your sit-rep?"

Bett responded amid a barrage of weapons fire in the background.

"We're running out of real estate, Raul. They've thrown the whole cudfrucking town at us."

I thought of the giant barantha trees dotting the hillside and the defensive positions they offered.

"Are you pinned down?"

"We're holding a line fifty meters from the stream. Been trying to punch a hole through their defenses, but they're blocking access. Twenty of these shits rappelled over the walls under heavy cover fire. Who in ten hells are these people?"

OK then. We were dealing with a town of commandos, not shepherds. Ixoca understated their ability when he called them guardians. I muted the comm and turned to Moon:

"If our new friend is right, we can do this ourselves. Game?"

"You know my answer."

I slapped my old pal on the shoulder.

"Nice." I tapped open the comm and told Bett: "They're more equipped and well-trained than I was informed. No worries. We have an ace in the hole, Stopper. Retreat to the ridgeline and hook up with Team 2."

"Negative, Raul. Team 2 is halfway down the valley. They were forced to advance to natural cover after taking heavy drone fire."

That explained why we detected no drones en route; the town held them in reserve.

"Elian, your status?"

"We're in trouble, boss. Genoa got a direct hit on a drone and took it down, but three more just launched from town, and there's a team of fighters advancing along the southern ridge."

"It's a noose," Bett said. "Soon as they're in position, they'll tighten till we can't breathe."

"Exactly why you must retreat. Ilan and I can handle them."

"What? How?"

"No, boss. Don't try it. You ain't gonna ..."

"Silence, my friends."

Our elevator reached the top floor. We jumped off and stared at a solid wall of rock with patterns matching the other entry.

"We'll be right behind you," I continued. "Team 1, retreat to Team 2's current position. Team 2, provide cover fire. When you hook up, dispatch Bart. Elian, take out the incoming drones but keep my sedan at a safe distance from ground fire. We'll need a way home. Yes?"

"S-sure, boss. I'm on it. Linking to Bart's remote Nav."

"Excellent. Raul, out. See you momentarily."

Now, to penetrate solid rock ...

"I'd have thought it would open automatically," Moon said. "This has to be Ixoca's secret exit."

"Of course. Secret exit for a secret lair. Fitting. I'm going to take a wild guess and say we already hold the key in our hands."

I held up my right, where tiny worms of blue light coursed under the epidermis.

"It's that simple?" Moon asked.

"I believe it is. You have the honor."

Moon placed his hand against the rock, which slid away. Another pocket door.

Just inside, we passed the top of the staircase and approached the original entry. Before we opened it with the same ease, I studied my pom. I counted four guardians at the T and three more halfway along our exit route.

"This door took three seconds to slide open last time. As soon as they hear it, they'll redirect their weapons."

"We can handle them, Royal."

"I like our odds, but Ixoca said nothing about the merger granting us immunity from laser bolts. He gave us a new weapon. Let's start there and see what mischief awaits."

"Whatcha got in mind, partner?"

When I told him my plan, Moon reacted like a kid with a shiny new toy. If I was right – and Ixoca kept his promise – a whole new world of opportunity was about to open. If not, well, a good old fashioned firefight wasn't a bad substitute.

We took opposite sides of the tunnel, stationed in corners which spelled ambush. I placed my right hand on the door, and it responded in perfect pocket fashion. Each of us aimed a rifle and waited for the first timid faces to cross the threshold.

We intended to finish our enemy in a manner to which we were unaccustomed, which made this ambush dicey. Yet now seemed a good time to test Ixoca's promised skillset. If it didn't work instantly, we'd rely upon traditional firepower.

Just like the sparkles along the shaft, humans were powered by an energy constructed at the molecular level. If we turned it off ...

Damn, what a concept.

I heard their footsteps, felt their heartbeats, and adjusted my optical sensors to penetrate their bodies. Ixoca whispered the rest: All I needed was direct line of sight.

The rest happened in not much more than a blink of an eye.

Two white-clothed gunmen entered the open door, their rifles leading the way. Were they terrified to cross a forbidden threshold? Might they have thought better of it if wiser counsel was nearby?

They should have run.

I couldn't see inside them like a medical scanner, but their organic matrix flashed into my mind's eye. I heard trillions of corpuscles hurrying through the bloodstream in a race that ended only at death. Healthy cells. Youthful, exuberant, warm, and red.

The Jewel's core matrix understood the molecular structure of all life forms. It spoke to me.

Then it demonstrated how to alter cellular development with an unspoken language programmed into the Jewels of Eternity by their creators, the J'Hai. The Jewels used this tool to wipe out the J'Hai before they embarked on a long, interstellar road in search of redemption. The tool showed me how to send a simple command.

I terraformed a human body.

The aorta's cellular structure unraveled, its muscular tissue deteriorated, and an entire world fell out of synchronicity.

The dam burst.

The male guardian nearest to me gagged and collapsed. The woman to his left and nearest to Moon spit blood and fell face-first onto the stone floor. Their eyes stared into nothing.

Quick and quiet perfection.

There wasn't time to consider the implications, but murder without firing a shot, slicing a blade, or planting a bomb?

We were playing a new game.

God style.

The other guardians didn't follow the dead through that doorway. One shouted to stand back, that Ixoca forbid them to cross.

They should've reached that conclusion a tad sooner.

The rest was simple, as I predicted to Moon.

Two guardians, stunned by what they saw, were not prepared when we surged into the opening like a blur. Our rifles cut them to pieces.

Next, we scurried along the main access to the outside world, hitting a wave of three guardians while their haphazard laser bolts zoomed by us. At the drain's exit, we took stock of the combat zone.

The guardians who had not yet crossed the stream to chase my teams heard the gunfire inside the drain and doubled back. I counted seven on approach. All this I saw without benefit of the goggles.

Nighttime was no longer an obstacle. The world appeared cast beneath the silver pumps of a full moon.

I chuckled.

"Guardians to the left of them, guardians to the right of them. Boldly they rode and well into the jaws of death. Into the mouth of hell rode the newly risen gods."

Moon got the message. He pointed to the four approaching from his flank, and I focused on the three nearing from mine. We lowered our rifles and called upon our new skillset.

I heard the heartbeats.

One. Two. Three.

I didn't perceive humans. They were evolutionary sculptures endowed with trillions of highly specialized but likewise fragile cells.

With a single command, I laid them down.

In a way, the new weapon showed mercy. There was no pain, no searing heat from a laser strike, no convulsion after being shredded by flash pegs or a bomb's shrapnel. No, these people exited without a shred of discomfort.

A shiny new toy indeed.

From the stream's edge, we evaluated the battlefield. Above us, blue and green laser bolts blasted from ramparts along the stone wall. Two lines of guardians advanced against my teams. The first pursued Bett's Team 1, slowed by covering fire from Elian's Team 2. Another set flanked my people, advancing along the steep slope of the hillside. Three drones with searchlights showered the valley. Streams of flickering flash pegs and yellow bolts rose from my teams' positions. All forces had converged except Bart.

Moon and I used a shorthand we developed centuries ago to plot our strategy. I opened the comm.

"Elian, where's Bart?"

He cursed. "Don't understand it, boss. I control the Nav, but it won't let me access weapons."

"Where is Bart?"

"Holding at a safe distance, like you ordered."

I'd scold Bart's AI afterward. Of all the times to cause trouble.

"Never mind. Leave it stationary. Teams 1 and 2, direct all fire at the drones. Bring them down. We'll handle the enemy."

Bett jumped in.

"The fuck are you? Mad?"

"Be there soon. Follow orders. Raul, out."

Moon grinned. "She thinks we're insane."

"When were we not, my friend?"

"Good point, partner. Ready?"

"Oh, yes. You go high, I'll go low."

"On it."

I leaped across the stream and set upon the enemy. I wanted to kill them all with a thought command, but their line was too wide to get a handle on everyone at once. Sorting through simultaneous internal mechanisms proved confusing.

Distance also confounded me. How far did line of sight work with this weapon? The first command I sent had no apparent effect. Only after I surged within twenty meters did my first victims fall.

By then, they responded to my rearguard assault.

I went down the line, blending my exceptional military training, speed they couldn't match, and Ixoca's gift.

Down, down, down.

Behind me, Moon dealt with cover fire spilling from the ramparts. Standing at the stream's edge, he took out each guardian who exposed himself for even a second. Moon didn't fire a shot.

What joy he must've felt. Moon always loved a good slaughter. And now? To make it so personal ...

Needless to say, the team of guardians advancing from the southern end of the valley had no chance against our combined precision. We obliterated them – most died from a ruptured blood vessel, exploding heart, or a brain aneurysm. I learned quickly to vary my targets.

As we took out the last enemy not hiding behind the walls, my teams shattered the last drones and rushed toward the ridgeline.

We heard confused, desperate shouts from town, and glow lights scattered in a chaotic symphony. Before we rendezvoused with our people, I thought briefly of Horatio Vargas's son, the saucer-eyed boy who returned my weapon and pom. Did he lay dead on this piss-poor battlefield? Did we take him down inside the drains or along the rampart? If so, how would his father respond? Ixoca said fallen eyes would motivate his people, but I didn't share his confidence.

Eh. Questions to face down the road.

We met our teams at the ridgeline. Which is to say, we shocked the holy hell out of them. They aimed in our direction when they heard rushing footsteps. Yeah, no. I should've warned them we were coming in hot. Might have been awkward had someone fired.

It was quite a moment. Elian, Ship, and Genoa smiled with relief but no great surprise. I was glad to see the kid made it. Stopper, Tracer, and Inky were slack-jawed and generally incredulous. In other words, the way any humans not in the loop would have logically responded.

"What happened out there?" Bett said. "Did you ...?"

"All done," I replied. "Good to see everyone's still with us. Sorry we took so long. Complicated, don't you know."

Bett threw off her goggles.

"The enemy died in seconds. How?"

I shared a fleeting glance with Moon, who nearabout burst.

"For starters, Ilan and I are faster than we appear. And we're very good shots. The rest, we'll speak to in Desperido. Elian, bring Bart in for a pickup. Hopefully, he'll do that much for us."

"Yes, boss. No worries."

"Good. There's a hornet's nest inside that town. Those lunatics will regroup and try again very soon, I suspect."

Tracer stood gingerly on his right leg, arm resting on Inky.

"Were you shot, Tracer?"

"Grazed. I'll live."

"Perfect, because I wouldn't want you to miss our celebration. Drinks all around in the cantina!"

Bart swung in close but unable to land at this treacherous angle. My gorgeous little sedan, who was very naughty tonight, hovered close enough that we could jump through the starboard egress.

Bett wasn't having it, though. Before we entered, she demanded an answer to one crucial question.

"I don't know what in the ten hells went on down there, but did you at least get what you came for?"

Now seemed like as good a time as any.

"Indeed we did."

I held up my right hand, which glowed with pieces of Ixoca.

"The fuck is that?"

"For you? It's seventy thousand credits tonight. But that's a drop in the ocean, my friend. Your lives will never be the same. I'll explain everything in due course."

I shared a wink with Elian, Ship, and Genoa, who winked in kind.

This felt like a perfect night to put on my dancing shoes.

## 22

CIGAR SMOKE FILLED THE CANTINA. The eight of us celebrated, though only Moon and I knew why. Of course, survival was ample reason to let loose, and my teams wouldn't have outlasted those guardians much longer. I underestimated the fanaticism – and resources – within Todos Santos. If Ixoca had that kind of pull on his children, his cult might have a fighting chance, after all.

Ship had never been so loud. Apparently, his stomach found a brand of whiskey it could process without discomfort. He recounted every minute of the adventure for my benefit. The kid claimed to have taken down one of the enemy and a drone, although the liquor did cloud his memory a bit. Genoa and Elian played along with patronizing smiles.

Maybe he'd grow into a proper assassin after all.

Eh. Long road ahead on that score.

The subject of what Moon and I found beneath the town never came up, round after round of drinks. I made it clear when we landed: Savor tonight's escape and meet in Bart after sunrise. There, I'd tell them a story they might have a hard time believing.

Well, not my lieutenants.

Stopper, Tracer, and Inky required a delicate approach. They carried out this mission in search of quick credits. It was a one-off.

Were they willing to commit to another war? A fulltime return to soldiering? Were they prepared to close the books on their old lives and enjoy a bright new future as murderers and cutthroats?

Honor was a fickle bitch. It had no price when the cause was just and the ideals were noble. But the institutions these three fought to preserve had betrayed them. That made Bett Ortiz, Geraldo Tolan, and Iago Sisal perfect candidates to leave the established order and pursue a reign of chaos.

We drank, joked, shared tales, and brought much needed life to this old cantina until deep into the night.

Suddenly, the mood changed. Moon sat across from me, facing the door. His laughter — something I heard for the first time since we arrived in Desperido — disappeared, replaced by a stone face. His eyes tracked someone behind me.

I knew who it was before I glanced over my shoulder. Minutes earlier, I noticed we lost a barkeep. Perhaps she'd gone inside her quarters to take a short break.

No. Lumen was walking out, a pouch slung over her shoulder.

"Going somewhere?" Moon shouted.

She eyed us with the usual disdain, and I thought she was preparing a witty retort. Instead, she opened the door and walked into the night. Huh.

"If you'll excuse me," I told our party. "Stopper, our bottle's nearabout empty. Surprise us."

Bett tucked her cheroot between her lips and pushed out her chair with command.

"On it."

Like many humans built with a heavy supply of assholery, Bett lightened up into a downright friendly and cooperative soul when properly sauced.

Yep. She'd come around to our vision.

As for Lumen? I found her on the central avenue walking north at a casual pace.

"So, are you leaving or throwing a temper tantrum?"

Moon joined us on Lumen's opposite flank.

"What's this about?" He asked.

She ignored us, so I took a different tact.

"You intend to walk Roadway 9 to Machado?" After no response, I added: "If that's the plan, you can hop a ride on Bart. We'll have you there in a jiffy."

Lumen didn't slow her pace, but I did strike a nerve.

"I'll walk barefoot in the desert before I accept a favor from you."

"Harsh, Lumen. I'm hurt. At the very least, wait until the morning and call for a transport."

"I won't stay in this town another hour."

"Well, I suppose if walking is your preference, it's cooler at night. Still, you packed water, I assume?"

She stifled a laugh.

"Don't pretend you care now, Raul. You wanted me gone weeks ago. How many times did you malgados talk about killing me?"

I glared at Moon, who shrugged.

"What do you think, partner? Ten? Fifteen?"

"At least," Moon said.

"But we reached the same conclusion every time, Lumen. No one runs the cantina as well as you."

"Bullshit, Raul. You kept me alive while I was useful. It had nothing to do with the cantina."

I could've grabbed her by the shoulder and swung her around.

Eh. Lumen deserved better. We stole everything she cared for.

"Experience matters, my friend. So do contacts. Between the Horax and the Children of Orpheus, you've been enormously useful. Who says you won't be tomorrow and beyond?"

She shot me the ol' side-eye while maintaining her pace.

"I knew I was finished the moment I handed you the truncator. There's nothing left to take, Raul."

"There you might be wrong."

She sighed, as if waiting for a lousy punchline.

"Go ahead. Kill me. It's what you assholes do best."

"True. Our skillset in that profession is exceptional. But I fail to see what purpose your death will serve. We own the town and everything in it. We've secured a brilliant future for all those who wish to follow our lead. And tonight, we acquired a special gift."

Lumen scoffed. "Can't you tell, Raul? I don't care. Either kill me or let me on with my business."

I threw up my hands and gave her space.

"Of course, of course. But the least you can do is tell me why you chose to leave tonight. What changed?"

She stopped and turned. On this subject, apparently, Lumen had something to say.

"What changed, you ask? Is that a serious question? Raul, what changed is that the cantina is booming. My liquor order has never been bigger. I am exhausted every night."

"That's a complaint? Sounds like superb economics to me. Good thing I added Bett to your pay stamp."

Lumen laughed in my face.

"These people – no, *your* people now – come in day and night to celebrate their good fortune. And they drink until all they can do is crawl home. Prosperity will kill these people. You are turning them into the worst version of a world they escaped. It was never like that before you two snakes came in from the desert. I won't watch it happen. Not another day. You can preside over its death."

She resumed her walk, no doubt feeling a pound or two lighter.

"That's it?" Moon said. "The woman who provides the liquor is worried about the drunks?"

Nice one.

Lumen, however, didn't miss a beat.

"I kept this town alive for thirty years. We never had much, but we sustained each other. I looked after them. They had a home. Now? You'll destroy these people. In a few months, Desperido will be an empty shell. A hole in the desert. I'm done."

Hard to argue. Given the changing landscape and our interstellar ambition, Lumen wasn't far off. Desperido's gold rush would end much sooner than later.

"You've always been free to leave, Lumen. We won't stop you. Just one last question: What's next? Youth is not on your side."

Yes, a cruel blow perhaps. But she literally abandoned her duties in the middle of the night.

"I haven't thought ahead, Raul. Perhaps I'll see my grandchildren, if I find them. Maybe I'll walk into a constabulary and tell them exactly what's really going on in this town. Or maybe I'll disappear off the grid again. Anyway I cut it, there will be two less demons in my life."

We crossed the town's internal defense perimeter. I knew now she wasn't full of bluster. Yesenia "Lumen" Rodriguez would never set foot in Desperido again.

Unless we gave her no choice, of course.

"Naturally, Lumen, we're sorry it didn't work out. Send us your new address, and we'll write."

Moon and I shared a chuckle. Assholery was a refined artform among the true masters.

We stopped following her. Moon whispered:

"She knows too much."

"True. But she doesn't care anymore. Who will believe her?"

"Only takes one."

"She's seen our defenses in action. She won't risk sending anyone else to their death."

Amid our debate about whether to silence a loose thread, Lumen surprised us. She swung around.

"Oh, there's one thing you can do. Think of it as small compensation in light of all you've stolen."

"Of course, Lumen. Anything."

"It's about Ship. The boy should be told the truth. I was planning to do it soon, but you stole his heart and mind."

Huh. Interesting.

"What truth?"

"He told you that his family exiled him from Everdeen for betraying them to the authorities."

"Yes. They were engaged in The Trade. He said you bought him on the night market."

"That's not how it happened. His family sent him offworld for protection. The true instigators were ruthless. They didn't accept his loss of a limb as sufficient payment. They marked him for death. I had paid in advance for off-book commodities, but when I met the dealer, he handed over the boy instead."

"Quite a mix-up."

"If I had rejected the boy, he would've been spaced on the next ship out. That's how those people worked."

Fascinating. Almost sounded like a final confession before dying. Did she know what might happen next?

"Why tell *us*, Lumen?"

"Because Ship is going to die anyway. You two will get him killed. Of that, I'm certain. I don't want him to leave this life believing his family tossed him away by choice. Tell him the truth."

"Absolutely. As soon as he's sober."

With that, she reverted to her northern course and said not another damn word.

We watched Lumen pass the exterior defense perimeter, a lonely and sad creature.

"Think we should have told her about Ixoca?" Moon asked.

"I considered it for about three seconds. No."

"Why not? She's a believer."

"She'd lose all faith if she knew Ixoca was our bosom buddy. It would've been one more thing we stole."

"Agree. Still, Royal. She's an angry cunt. I wouldn't put it past her to tell the wrong people about us."

My partner was right, of course. We'd soon be entering a phase of high risk/reward propositions. Did we need a wildcard like Lumen roaming Azteca? I had to admit: I was torn.

She cared about the kid. So did I. An execution on a dark desert road seemed unfair at best.

"Tell you what," I told Moon. "The choice is yours. If you decide she needs to go, I ask one thing, my friend. Quick and painless."

Lumen's odds to survive the night fell off a cliff.

"It will be like the guardians, Royal. She won't feel it."

"Good. I'll leave you to consider the options."

"And you, partner?"

I gazed at the stars and considered the many adventures which lay ahead. Then thought of the immediate, practical need.

"I'll ask if anyone's interested in fulltime barkeep."

"Good luck with that."

Yeah, no. Somebody had to manage that bastard. Otherwise, we'd have alcohol anarchy. That would indeed send us straight down the road Lumen predicted.

Bett was the natural choice, of course, but I suspected we needed a new approach. A team. Like normal businesses.

Manager, assistant manager, team leader, associates.

And why not? After all, I intended to create a clear and undisputed hierarchy when our army took to space, spreading discord, drug addiction, and death wherever possible.

Best I practice now.

I was about to reach for the cantina door when Moon caught up with me. I glanced up the long, black road.

"Did you kill her already?"

He chuckled, which was strange. Moon never chuckled.

"She can't hurt us. Plus, that road is a hell of a lot longer on foot than she thinks."

I gigged my partner in his so-called ribs.

"Oh, you old softie. I'll have to file a report."

"To whom and for what?"

I shrugged. "I'll spread the word to every homicidal maniac, serial killer, and plague spreader from here to Earth: Moon the Serpent God shows mercy."

His jaw hardened, but I knew he didn't mean it.

"Go ahead. They're all amateurs."

"For the most part. Some will be our employees one day."

"We can hope."

We entered the cantina and rejoined the celebration, fending off those annoying questions about the barkeep.

Smoking, drinking, and laughing continued deep into the night. It was a brilliant prelude.

First thing the next morning, we talked about the future, about gods and assassins, and about the war we intended to unleash.

..........

The saga continues now in Book 4: Black Star.